MIDNIGHT

A NOVEL BY
TOM CLAFFEY

ISBN: 978-1-59152-218-8

For more information or to order extra copies of this book
call Farcountry Press toll free at (800) 821-3874.

sⱳeetgrassbooks

Produced by Sweetgrass Books
PO Box 5630, Helena, MT 59604; (800) 821-3874;
www.sweetgrassbooks.com

 Produced and printed in the United States of America.

22 21 20 19 18   1 2 3 4 5

Also by Tom Claffey

To
Gayle, Kathleen, and Marilyn

"The West is a special place."

GOVERNOR MATTHEW H. MEAD,
GOVERNOR, THE STATE OF WYOMING.
FROM HIS WELCOME REMARKS TO THE
WESTERN WRITERS OF AMERICA,
CHEYENNE, WYOMING, JUNE 23, 2016.

1

THE HILL COUNTRY IN THE SOUTH-CENTRAL PORTION OF THE LONE STAR State is particularly beautiful in the fall season with its rolling grasslands, white limestone cliffs, fat Texas Longhorns, and gold, yellow, and red colored foliage. During two days of pickups and deliveries in and around Austin in early October 2015, Kelsey Brannigan absorbed it all from the cab of her red Peterbilt 18-wheeler. Atop the front of the hood stood a chrome rubber duck given to her by C.W. McCall years earlier during a layover in Ouray, Colorado, his hometown. C.W. McCall, revered composer of the truckers' anthem, "Convoy."

Checklist completed, she had left Austin before sunrise on a Wednesday morning and headed home to Corrales, a suburb of Albuquerque. The fifty-two-foot trailer held a shipment of lab equipment from the College of Natural Sciences at the University of Texas to be delivered to Atchison Industries in Albuquerque. The shipment, strapped down and secured, occupied about half the space in the trailer.

The predawn traffic was light and oncoming vehicles kept their headlights on low beam, which Kelsey appreciated. She found most early-morning drivers to be relaxed and attentive as opposed to the stressed-out, angry crowd of late afternoon or early evening.

During one long stretch in Travis County, while it was still dark, she counted three shooting stars.

In her mid-thirties, Kelsey wore a dark brown Stetson, her sun-glasses, wrapped around the front of the crown, resting on the brim. She'd be putting the glasses on soon with the arrival of bright morning sun. Among truckers, Kelsey was known as *Bronco Brannigan*. More about that later.

Weaving through the hills and ranchlands between Briggs and Lometa, the big rig's wheels beat a steady drumbeat against the seams of the concrete two-lane highway. Thick-a-thunk, thick-a-thunk, thick-a-thunk. A few miles north of Briggs, two deer shot across the highway, their brown coats almost a blur in the headlights. Too close. Way too close. She took a deep breath and glanced skyward. "Thank you, God."

In Clovis, she would gas up and load three dozen wooden pallets in the empty half of the trailer for delivery in Santa Rosa.

Kelsey gripped the top of the steering wheel with her gloved hands while her elbows rested on the sides. The gloves' worn black calfskin concealed months and miles of oil and grease stains.

In the passenger seat, beside Kelsey, stood her driving partner Max, a tan- and white-haired mutt with terrier and schnauzer lineage plus whatever ancestors may have jumped over the back fence along the way. She found the dog on Christmas Eve 2012, curled up and shivering behind a trash can at a central Oklahoma truck stop during an emergency run for a hospital supply company. She named him Maximus. Never knew why. The name just seemed to fit. She later shortened it to Max. He wasn't a big dog, but he was feisty and fiercely protective.

Her black ponytail settled against the collar of her long-sleeved khaki shirt. With the first splash of sunrise, she reached up for the wraparound glasses and put them on, hiding her blue eyes and distinctive crow's feet, chevrons earned from twelve years of trucking—five years with the U.S. Army in Iraq and Fort Bragg and seven years driving for her dad's trucking company in Seattle.

Kelsey grew up in Tukwila, Washington, near Seattle, where she and her older brother, Paul, drove for Brannigan Trucking. Her dad, Pops Brannigan, ran the business and maintained their three 18-wheelers. He also drove from time to time. Kathleen Brannigan, her mom, took care of the office.

Kelsey and Paul were close, closer than most siblings they knew. Nonetheless, she was always the little sister, he the big brother. When they drove together as a team, Paul was the boss. They covered Washington, Oregon, and British Columbia together until Paul got married and started a family. He soon discontinued the long-haul runs and stuck to routes closer to home.

About the time she was beginning to enjoy her independence, Kelsey, then in her early twenties, joined an Army National Guard transportation unit, which shortly afterwards was activated and deployed to Iraq.

Pops Brannigan, a Vietnam veteran and former Army Ranger, gave his little girl a hug and a salute before she left. He then took over her route.

Kelsey glanced back as Pops blew his nose then lit a Marlboro cigarette and strapped on his back brace and climbed into her rig. The brace was the result of a fall off a loading dock several months earlier.

The Iraq War, which began in 2003 and "ended" in 2011, claimed 4,500 Americans killed and 32,000 wounded, touching every part of America.

Kelsey's unit deployed in 2005. She was a PFC truck driver, a private first class. Drove the big ones, 5-ton cargo trucks and, occasionally, heavily laden flatbeds. In 2011, six years later, she received an honorable discharge with the rank of staff sergeant.

She returned home bearing no physical scars. Her psychological scars were another matter. Emotional wounds of death, of loss, of finding the strength to carry a fellow driver from his burning truck, rescuing an Iraqi child from the midst of horrific crossfire during an ambush. Brain-searing images of casualties from improvised explosive devices (IEDs) never left her. Kelsey Brannigan knew when it was time to leave, to decline another enlistment and return home—to Pops and her red Peterbilt rig. She had worn her Army uniform with pride and would wear it again if she was asked to.

"Deep, deep down in my heart," she told her dad one day when he was working on the engine of one of the rigs, "I knew the war was necessary." She was sitting on the concrete floor of the maintenance bay, her chin resting on her folded arms. "Being around the Iraqi people as I was, and seeing how oppressed they were was traumatic. They weren't able to fight for themselves. I'm glad we were there." Her voice wavered. "But, Pops, it was the children! The poor children."

Pops stepped down to the floor, lifted his daughter, and wrapped his strong arms around her.

"You saw the children in Vietnam, didn't you?" She felt him nod.

"I know there's more to all this than I'll ever understand," she murmured, her head resting against his chest. "Aren't there other ways to settle differences?" She sighed and caught her breath. "Sometimes at night I wake up crying . . . and I can't go back to sleep."

He tightened his hold.

Six months later Pops Brannigan died. Lung cancer. Kelsey was at a loss. She loved her mother, but she adored her Pops. And she missed him.

Kelsey continued to drive during the next several months while she and Paul downsized Brannigan Trucking until all that remained was Paul and his Kenworth 350. She kept her Peterbilt and sold her remaining interest in the family business to Paul. Their mother, Kathleen, moved in with a cousin in Tacoma.

Someone told her of a trucking company in Albuquerque, Doc Morgan Trucking, a company run by a woman driver, Sally Tremaine, former businesswoman turned cattle rancher turned trucker. Soon thereafter, Kelsey Brannigan and Sally Tremaine, both strong-minded, independent women, met at an Albuquerque restaurant for a dinner of green chile enchiladas and margaritas. They hit it off from the start.

Thick-a-thunk, thick-a-thunk, thick-a-thunk. Leaving Abilene and continuing west, Kelsey's mind drifted again to her time as an Army trucker—to Jesse Harper, her almost-fiancé. Kind, handsome Jesse. They found a special kinship, she and Jesse, thousands of miles away from home. Both were seasoned truckers before their Army days and both came from tight-knit, supportive families. Returning stateside together, they soon realized things were not going to work out with Jesse wanting a large family with lots of kids and Kelsey not yet being ready. They slowly drifted apart. She wondered if he was still in the Army. Probably a master sergeant by now.

The constantly changing Texas landscape transitioned from cotton fields to herds of cattle to wind farms, then oil field pump jacks. Some of the locals referred to the jacks as *nodding donkeys*.

Kelsey was reminded of another Texas run, some years back, when she checked into a Best Western motel on the outskirts of San Angelo. She was by herself—that was before Max—when she decided, instead of a truck-stop meal, to treat herself to dinner at an eatery, Jack's Steaks and Bar-B-Que, not far from the motel.

The restaurant, she was told, was a real cowboy hangout with great food and filled with friendly locals and out-of-towners. She put on one of her old cowboy hats and headed to Jack's.

She was seated at a small table at the edge of the dining area, beside a circular table with a lean middle-aged woman and three cowboys. Empty beer bottles were neatly arranged near the center of the table, which seemed to be under the command of the woman. Though she probably didn't weigh much more than a hundred pounds, Kelsey sized her up right away as the boss. Their chairs were close enough that Kelsey could look down and see the woman's worn, dusty boots. There were spurs on the boots. Lots of razzing and laughter going on around the table. The cowboys drank beer and the boss lady drank iced tea. Kelsey ordered a glass of merlot.

The woman turned. "You from around here?"

"No, ma'am, I'm from Corrales, New Mexico."

"You a rancher?"

"I'm a trucker."

"Come on, now." The woman tilted her head. "Are you really?"

"Yes, ma'am. A gear-jammin' honest-to-God woman trucker." Kelsey smiled. "You're looking at her."

"We're in need of a trucker."

The three cowboys listened to the conversation, and one of them stood and pulled another chair to the table beside the boss lady. "We can't have you eating by yourself," he said as he tipped his hat. "Come on over and join us." He appeared to be the oldest with his graying hair and unshaven face.

"Heavens, yes," the lady said, and patted the chair. "Please have a seat."

"Why, thank you," Kelsey said. She picked up her napkin and silverware with the glass of merlot and moved to their table, sitting between the woman and the bearded cowboy.

The woman held out her hand. "I'm Patty Wilson."

"Kelsey Brannigan." Kelsey shook her hand.

"And these are my three ranch hands." She swept her hand around the table.

Kelsey stretched out and shook hands with the three cowboys.

"They're also my sons," Patty continued, "and all three of them are single." She tapped her glass of iced tea against Kelsey's merlot and laughed. "You married?"

The three men joined in the laughter until the older one, sitting beside Kelsey, said, "Come on now, Mom. Slow down. She just got here." More laughter.

The cowboy Kelsey guessed to be the middle brother chimed in. "I think you found yourself with a wild bunch, Kelsey. The Wilson boys can get kinda rowdy sometimes."

"I'm not worried, boys. I can take care of myself." She felt Patty's hand on her back giving her a pat. "I have a hunch you can, Kelsey." Patty waved to the waitress who came to take their orders.

Patty ordered chicken fried steak and fried okra. Kelsey ordered prime rib. The men each ordered steak.

Patty dug into her meal with fierce determination. Kelsey noticed her dry, tired face, deep crow's feet etched beside her eyes—a hardworking gal with lots of miles and lots of hours in the saddle. She glanced away when the woman picked her teeth with her fingernails and wiped her hands on her Levis.

After their plates were eaten clean, Patty leaned in to Kelsey. "Like I said earlier, I'm in need of a trucker. You ever hauled cattle?"

"Pulled a bull wagon? Yeah, a time or two."

"Want a job working for us?"

"No thanks, Patty. I have a good driving job in Albuquerque."

Patty's smile disappeared. "Suit yourself."

The baby-faced brother, with two rows of dirty teeth and a silly grin, interrupted from the other side of the table. "Maybe you could marry one of us, Kelsey." He belched. "Like me."

"Excuse me?" Kelsey frowned.

"Marry me and we could all share."

"What do you mean?"

"Us Travis boys share everything." As he spoke, saliva began to gather in the corners of his mouth. "Marryin' one of us would be like marryin' all of us! We could all share you."

The three men laughed.

"That's what I mean." He belched again.

Kelsey turned to Patty, awaiting a reprimand from mother to sons.

Patty grinned at Kelsey and shrugged. "Boys will be boys."

Kelsey's stomach turned. She reached into her pocket and pulled out a twenty-dollar bill. She tossed it on the table. "You people are sick."

The older brother seated beside Kelsey placed his hand on her wrist. "You can't talk to us like that!" He tightened his grip.

"Let go of the girl, Hiram," Patty scowled. "Now!"

He released his hold and his mother reached for the twenty and handed it to Kelsey. "Dinner's on me."

Kelsey tossed it back on the table, stood, and walked out of the café, then drove back to the motel, checked out, and got back on the road.

She stopped in Clovis for the wooden pallets, which were loaded so quickly she barely had time to visit the restroom.

Further west, driving through a flat stretch of gray sage, she thought of the days and nights she and Paul drove together. The situations they'd encountered, the characters they met, and the security he provided. Now, driving solo, without heavyset, weight-lifting Paul at her back, she experienced occasional wisecracks from sharp-tongued truckers who resented intrusion from women drivers in the male-dominated industry. Max, the ever-scrappy protector, was quick to growl and raise a ruckus to level the playing field if he sensed a threat. Thick-a-thunk, thick-a-thunk.

Recently, during a break at a truck stop outside Pine Bluff, Arkansas, she and Max got out of the cab to do a quick tire check with a wooden tie thumper, a trucker device about the size of a small baseball bat. Beside her rig stood a refrigerated produce rig with an off-white tractor and a red trailer with California plates. Its driver, an overweight man with a three-day growth of beard and a grease-stained tank top, bumped against her, knocking her off balance as she leaned over one of the trailer's rear tires.

The skin above Max's nose curled as he bared his teeth and sent out a guttural warning.

"Out of my way, bitch," he mumbled.

No sooner were the words out of his mouth than Max jumped the guy from behind and ripped a new air vent in the seat of his pants as Kelsey whirled upward. "You son of a bitch!" she shouted, gripping the tire thumper in her right hand while Max snarled and stood his ground behind the hostile trucker.

A white-haired cowboy trucker had just parked his pumpkin-orange Schneider rig close by. He got out of his truck and headed toward the station.

"Hey, Schneider!" Kelsey yelled. "I need help!"

The white-haired trucker spun around and charged in her direction.

The fat guy took a step back. "You damned bitch," he snarled. "Get your goddamned dog away from me!" He kicked at Max and missed. "You women drivers got no fucking business driving these big rigs." He spat a chunk of tobacco on the ground. She noticed a black swastika tattooed on the back of his right hand.

Kelsey smelled the putrid odor of the yellowish-brown wad and grimaced. She did a quick glance toward the sound of heavy boots. The tall Schneider trucker approached and stepped between her and the loudmouth. He glanced at Kelsey. "What's the problem, lady?" He was a husky man with wavy white hair and a well-groomed moustache and beard. He wore an open leather vest and a faded cowboy hat.

"She got in my way!" the fat trucker sneered. "The crazy bitch!"

"I'm not talking to you, buddy." He turned back to Kelsey.

"I believe this arrogant bastard has a problem with lady drivers," Kelsey said in a low voice. "I'd love to kick his fat ass across the parking lot. Thanks for coming over."

Max kept his eyes on the loudmouth and stalked around to stand beside Kelsey. He raised his upper lip and growled again.

"She and her kind are taking our jobs." Tobacco juice dripped down the fat trucker's chin. He wiped it off with the palm of his hand. On his shoulder was another tattoo, *Sal*.

The Schneider trucker tipped his large cowboy hat to the back of his head and faced the loudmouth. "You better get used to it, buddy." He glanced at the shoulder. "Your name Sal?"

"Yeah. Sal Zimmer. So, what?"

"Women drivers are here to stay, Sal Zimmer." He reached out and twisted the man's tank top in his fist. They were the same height.

"My ass." The loudmouth spit a stream of tobacco juice on the ground.

Again, Kelsey smelled the stench.

The trucker tightened the twist until the fat man's eyes widened in fear. "Now, shithead," he said quietly, "I suggest you go about your business and let this lady and her dog go about theirs." He narrowed his eyes. "Are you understanding me?" He released his grip on the man's tank top and shoved him backwards. "Get the hell outa here."

The loudmouth began to speak, then changed his mind. He turned and walked back to his truck.

"Thank you." Kelsey held the white-haired man's eyes and leaned down to pet Max.

"You're welcome." He took off his gloves and shoved them in his back pocket. "Are you alright?"

She nodded. "I'm fine."

"Name's Bill Gentry. Also known as *Buffalo*." He held out his hand and grinned. "I ride in rodeos from time to time." He glanced over at his rig. "When I'm not drivin' the Big Orange."

She took his hand. "I'm Kelsey. Kelsey Brannigan." Then she smirked. "Buffalo Bill! I've heard of you! Also heard of Buffalo Bill Cody, of course. You actually look like him."

Gentry chuckled. "I'm glad you see the resemblance."

"I've heard your handle on the CB. Your *Buffalo* nickname. And I know your name on the rodeo circuit!"

He furrowed his brow. "Do *you* ride?"

"On a dare I jumped on a bronco in Laramie one time. Scared the hell out of me. I still do it every once in a while. Drives my mother up the wall."

"You ever made your eight seconds in the saddle?"

"Once."

"By any chance, are you *Bronco* Brannigan?"

Kelsey grinned. "I'm the one."

"Well, I'll be damned!" Buffalo laughed and shook his head. "What's your dog's name?"

"Maximus. I call him Max." Kelsey scratched Max's ear.

"That's a pretty big name for such a small dog."

"I suppose it is. But don't tell him." She grinned. "He thinks he's a big dog. And, if need be, he can be a scrapper."

"Let's you and me and Max go inside for a cup of coffee."

Thus began a friendship Kelsey put right up there near the top.

2

HALFWAY BETWEEN CLOVIS AND SANTA ROSA, KELSEY REACHED OVER AND patted Max. It was late in the day and they had covered a lot of miles since Austin. "There's a pull-off up here a short way. I think you and I are both due for a break, Max." Kelsey eased up on the gas pedal and dropped her hand to the gearshift knob. Traffic on the two-lane highway was light.

She brought the 18-wheeler to a stop in an asphalt parking area a short distance from the highway and kept the engine running while she and Max got out of the cab. He christened a few fence posts nearby while Kelsey performed a quick maintenance walk-around. After several minutes they got back in the rig and continued northwest.

Crosswinds buffeted the trailer. When the sun began to disappear behind a fast-moving bank of clouds, Kelsey took off her wraparound sunglasses and returned them to the brim of her Stetson. "Looks like we may hit some weather, Maxy." He was sitting in the passenger seat looking straight ahead. "Sure wish we had a heavier load. That stack of pallets we picked up in Clovis added no weight at all. The trailer's getting rambunctious back there." Heavy raindrops splashed against the windshield.

She slowed the rig and reached for the CB mic. "Break one-nine, this is Bronco Brannigan, westbound, highway eight-four between Clovis and Santa Rosa. Anybody near that storm sitting over Fort Sumner? Come on."

"Hey, Brannigan," came an immediate reply, "this is Smoky Joe, eastbound on eight-four heading toward Fort Sumner. It's comin' . . . pretty fierce . . . storm . . . hail . . ."

Kelsey pressed the mike key. "Smoky Joe, you're breaking up. Say again." There was no reply, only static. Kelsey knew Smoky Joe Lassiter. A family man with a wife and three kids from Gatlinburg, Tennessee in the Great Smoky Mountains and a devoted fan of the University of Tennessee Volunteers. A true southern gentleman. His daughter, Tess, had played basketball for Coach Pat Summitt some time back. He still wore the frayed orange *Vols* baseball cap she gave him after one of the games.

He drove a maroon Freightliner tractor with a white trailer for Knight Transportation. Kelsey and Smoky Joe chatted on the CB from time to time. Shortly after she began driving with Doc Morgan Trucking, she and Joe met at a horrific accident scene during a severe sandstorm on Interstate 8 in Arizona. Several rigs and 4-wheelers were involved. Together the two of them rescued a family of four trapped in a burning SUV.

Several months later, in mid-December, they visited over a cup of coffee during a chance encounter at a Denver truck stop while a Rocky Mountain blizzard raged outside, nearly burying the trucks in snow.

"We've got to quit meeting like this," Kelsey said to Smoky as the two of them sat on opposite sides of a community table. "It's either fire in Arizona or ice in Colorado."

"Fire or ice," Smoky chuckled and wrapped his bony hands around the hot coffee cup. "Interesting combination, Brannigan." He raised his head. "You know you shouldn't be driving alone, young lady. Especially in weather like this."

Kelsey sighed. "You sound like my mom."

"Well, your mom's right, dadgummit. You should at least have a dog riding with you. A big dog."

"One of these days I'll find one. But, don't worry, Smoky. I can take care of myself."

Two weeks later, on Christmas Eve, she found Max shivering behind the trash can in Oklahoma.

Like a blast from the bowels of the Arctic, a staccato of hailstones pummeled the Peterbilt on all sides. "Holy crap!" Kelsey shouted. "This is far more excitement than I would like to be having right now!" She reached down and tightened her seatbelt, then downshifted and checked both rearview mirrors for anyone behind her as she rounded a curve.

She thought a car was following her, but wasn't certain. Heavy rain and road grime nearly obliterated the surfaces of both outside mirrors. "I CAN'T SEE YOU, GODDAMMIT! TURN ON YOUR FUCKING HEADLIGHTS!" Visibility had dropped to less than fifty yards.

A late model sports car zoomed past her on the left. "ASSHOLE!" she shouted. She glanced at Max sitting on the passenger seat with apprehension in his eyes and his ears pinned back. She reached over and patted his neck.

"Taiban is just ahead. About three miles." She was talking to herself and to Max, as she often did. Her khaki shirt was turning dark with sweat and her left hand tightened on the steering wheel. Her right hand gripped the black-knobbed gearshift handle.

"Bronco," the speaker came back to life. "Smoky Joe here. What's your twenty?"

Kelsey keyed the mike. "Good to hear you, Smoky." She paused. "Maybe two miles east of Taiban."

"Roger. I just arrived Fort Sumner. Pulling up beside a restaurant on the main drag. There's a Super 8 Motel across the way." He paused. "This is a bad-ass weather system, Brannigan. Hope you don't run into it. I'm going to cash in and spend the night here."

"Understand. I see heavy lightning over your way."

"Young lady, you be careful." There was a pause. "Are you near a spot where you can pull off until this system passes?"

"Taiban is just ahead. I stopped there one time before." She hesitated. "Current visibility is terrible." There was a deafening thunder clap. "Thanks for your concern." A strong gust of wind slammed against the trailer.

"You got your dog with you?"

"He's sitting here in the passenger seat. Brannigan signing off."

"Take care of yourself, Kelsey. Ten-four."

The rig began to swerve. Kelsey tightened her grip on the wheel and downshifted when, a hundred yards ahead, she saw the faint outline of Taiban's abandoned Presbyterian Church.

Taiban was a small New Mexico town where Pat Garrett captured Billy the Kid in 1880. One year later, in July 1881, the Kid would be dead—killed by Garrett.

According to records Kelsey had read, the church was built in 1908.

She turned right onto a gravel road running alongside the old weathered building. Then, in the midst of tornado-force winds and with skill that would make her dad proud, she backed the big rig into a narrow gravel strip facing the highway. Rain, hail, and flying debris slammed against the semi, flashing her mind back to gunfire in Iraq. She turned off the engine and reached across the seat to Max. He licked her hand and returned his attention to the hail and debris hammering the windshield.

They sat for another half hour, listening to the National Weather Station in Albuquerque urging anyone near the storm cell to get off the highway and seek shelter. The storm intensified to an ear-shattering peak, then weakened. After several minutes it moved on.

Kelsey took a deep breath and reached to her pocket where, a few years earlier, she'd have found a pack of Camels. "Max, I could use a smoke right now." She cracked the window an inch or so. The cool air was refreshing.

A few random raindrops pinged off the skin of the cab. Then it was quiet. And dark.

"Let's get out and stretch." Kelsey scratched Max's ear, then reached for the handle and opened the door to the silence of prairie nighttime. She stepped to the ground and into a shallow puddle of water surrounded by hailstones. She reached back and lifted Max out of the truck. His paws hit the soggy ground and he shot out of her hands through scattered storm debris to a mesquite bush. "Wish I could pee that quick and easy," she quipped.

She walked around the rig with a flashlight, checking the truck and trailer for damage. There were a few dents and dings, nothing else. More would be visible in daylight. She stretched and gazed skyward at stars and planets beginning to peek through scattered storm clouds.

After a few minutes she returned to the cab and retrieved Max's aluminum water pan and filled it with water. Then she put some dog food in another pan and placed both pans in a sheltered area beneath the trailer. Max dug right in. When he was finished, they got back in the cab.

Kelsey locked the doors and they adjourned to the sleeper cab behind the driver and passenger seats. The sleeper contained a tiny bathroom, a kitchenette, a narrow bunkbed, and storage accommodations. She prepared a light dinner meal for herself: macaroni and cheese with a small salad.

Two hours later, after eating and reading three chapters of a Johnny D. Boggs novel, she let Max out for a few minutes. When he barked at the door, she let him in and once again locked the cab doors, then crawled into the small bed, falling fast asleep. Max curled up on the floor beside her.

∽∽∽∽∽

A pair of eyes from beneath the abandoned wood-slatted church watched the semitruck parked out on the narrow strip of gravel. Rainwater had stopped dripping from holes in the warped wooden floor of the church. The eyes remained fixed on the truck cab. From the distance came a forlorn whistle from an eastbound locomotive.

3

FAINT EARLY MORNING LIGHT LINED THE EDGES OF THE INSULATED curtains covering the windshield and cabin doors. Kelsey rolled over in the cot-size bed and opened one eye. Max's chin rested on the edge of the mattress and their eyes locked on each other.

There was no deadline or delivery date to meet for the next three days. Sally Tremaine or Vicky Lovato, the trucking office manager, would contact her if anything urgent came up.

She reached out and scratched Max's ear. "You probably want to go outside, huh?" His tail thumped against the floor.

Kelsey swung her legs over the side and rubbed her eyes, then reached for her red flannel shirt and jeans. She stepped down into the cab and pulled back the curtains. The sky was clear with the morning star and Venus starting to fade. A solitary vehicle sped down the highway fifty yards away as she reached down and opened the driver's side door. She helped Max to the ground then got back in the cab and cracked the side windows and locked the doors.

After washing up, she stood in front of the vanity mirror tying a blue and white bandana around her hair. When she heard Max barking she stepped down into the cab and went outside. The area resembled what one would expect following a violent, tornadic storm, with vegetation and tree branches strewn about. A piece of side panel from the old church rested on the steel platform between the truck cab and the trailer. She glanced to where Max stood barking at something beneath the old church on the other side of the truck. He'd bark, then look back at her trying to get her attention.

She walked through the debris and around the truck to Max. In one hand she held a small Mace canister, as she always did in unfamiliar surroundings. In the other hand a flashlight to see into the dark area beneath the church.

She got down on the soaked gravel beside Max. "What is it, boy?"

He stared at the dark recess beneath the church and whined. His ears pointed forward. He whined again and began to prance with his front paws.

A sound came from the dark area. A subtle *quorking* sound. Max whined and Kelsey turned on the flashlight and shone it toward the sound.

It was a bird. A large black bird. A raven or a crow. It appeared to be injured, a victim of the nighttime storm. Kelsey inched closer. The bird was too large to be a crow. Must be a raven. Its right wing hung limply at its side. It looked at her and cocked its head, letting out a low murmur.

Kelsey moved the flashlight beam around the raven. It was resting on a piece of wood, part of the church floor, which had fallen to the ground and was surrounded by a pool of rainwater. "You poor thing," she said softly. "I'll try to help you."

Max pressed his nose forward. The bird didn't move. Neither creature seemed to fear the other.

"I'll bet you're hungry." Kelsey paused. "I wish I had a mouse or some worms for you. Or some yukky roadkill." She bit her lip. "What can I feed you?"

Max whined.

"Dog food! What about some dog food?" She reached out and patted Max.

While Max stood guard over the raven, Kelsey retrieved the narrow wood panel that had blown between the truck cab and the trailer and placed it on the ground near Max. She returned to the truck and opened a trailer side door and stepped up to grab a small canvas tarp. Then she went into the crew cab for a can of dog food. A few moments later she stepped down with half the can's contents on a paper plate.

She placed the plate on the end of the narrow panel. After spreading the tarp on the wet ground, she kneeled on it and reached forward to push the panel toward the injured bird. She withdrew her hands and sat back on her haunches. Max sat beside her.

The raven cocked its head to examine the dog food. It let out a low, barely audible *grunt*, then stretched forward and took a bite of dog food and gulped it down. Then another. And another.

"My God, you poor, dear creature," Kelsey said in a low voice, "you are *so* hungry." She rose to her feet. "I'm going to get the rest of the can. Max, you stay." He looked at her and wagged his tail, then returned his attention to the big black bird.

She surveyed the area as she walked back to the rig, not certain what she was looking for, but mentally recording every detail. There were still a few buildings standing in the old, almost ghost town a couple of blocks away. Some appeared to be occupied although she saw no one at this early morning hour. Lights from two ranch houses were visible in the distance.

A few minutes later she jumped down from the truck cab with the open can of dog food and returned to Max and the raven. They were still studying each other.

She had read that ravens were usually alone or in pairs, so she scanned the immediate area and listened for signs of a mate. There were none.

The raven was still resting on the piece of wood within easy reaching distance, a foot inside the area beneath the church.

It turned its head to Kelsey as she knelt once again and set down the dog food can. When she placed her hand on the strip of wood panel holding the paper plate, the bird made a few bill-snaps and watched as she carefully pulled the narrow panel with the empty paper plate toward her and scooped the remaining dog food onto the plate.

She reached into a shirt pocket for a dog biscuit and handed it to Max to distract him from the dog food. He got down on the tarp and began chewing it as she scooted toward the raven on her hands and knees while sliding the paper plate along the surface of the wood panel.

The raven watched her every move, but made no effort to retreat. Its injured right wing hung at its side. The distance between them slowly shortened. Kelsey eased the paper plate forward. It was just a few inches away from the raven.

She was close enough to reach out and touch the bird, but elected not to. She eased the plate to the bird's beak, then drew back her hand.

"I'm going to name you *Midnight*." She grinned. "Midnight, the Majestic Raven."

The raven let out a quiet *caulk*, then stretched forward once again for a chunk of dog food and swallowed it. He turned to Kelsey with a *grunt*.

She smiled. "You're welcome."

4

S ALLY TREMAINE AND DIXIE O'DONNELL, TEAM DRIVERS FOR DOC MORGAN
Trucking, watched the same sun beginning to break Wyoming's eastern
horizon that Kelsey, with Max and the raven, were seeing to the south in
New Mexico.

Sally tightened both her hands on the steering wheel. "Dix, look at
that magnificence! The early morning clouds with their folds of gray and
fiery orange."

"It's like a painting," Dix said softly.

Sally and Dixie, who preferred to go by Dix, had met a decade earlier in Santa Fe when they were both at a crossroads in their lives. Sally
had owned a successful cattle ranching operation on the Colorado/New
Mexico border for several years prior to selling it and moving to Santa Fe.
Dixie, a widow from Beaumont, Texas, had recently moved to a retirement facility in Santa Fe where her two sons owned a bicycle shop.

The two women met by chance at a real estate open house south of
town one Saturday afternoon and struck an immediate friendship. They
soon accepted the fact they were not yet ready to settle into rocking
chairs and, on an inspired whim, hired a licensed commercial trucker, Slim
Perkins, to teach them to drive an 18-wheeler.

Slim, whose given name was Eliot, had graduated from the University
of Texas with a degree in music. The tall, affable pianist was given the
nickname *Slim* at the university. After graduation he was accepted in the
Masters program at the Juilliard School in New York City. Before leaving
for Juilliard, however, he was caught in a nightclub fire in central Texas
where he was filling in for the club's permanent piano player. His hands
sustained severe damage from the fire, forcing him to give up music to
accept his father's offer to join him as a team driver on his 18-wheeler,
transporting building materials throughout central Texas. Slim mastered
the big rig skills and was subsequently hired as a trainer for a trucking company in Beaumont. Word of mouth through Dix's Beaumont

connections paved the way for his catching a bus to Santa Fe to train Dix and Sally in the ways of trucking.

After the two women passed the rigorous licensing exams and earned commercial driving licenses, they purchased a robin's egg-blue Kenworth 900 with a custom sleeper and became drivers for Doc Morgan, a retired physician, who invited them and Slim to join him as drivers for his new trucking company, Doc Morgan Trucking. They then became members of the Women in Trucking Association and never looked back.

∞∞∞∞∞

Rays of bright white morning light illuminated the cab as Sally pulled into the Broken Wheel Truck Stop in Douglas, Wyoming. They had driven through the night.

Tied down securely in the long trailer were several pieces of meticulously calibrated lab monitors from Atchison Industries, equipment similar to that delivered by Kelsey to the University of Texas. The shipment had been rushed through production for Eastern Wyoming College in Douglas to replace critically needed diagnostic monitors destroyed nine days previously from an electrical fire triggered by a freak lightning storm.

∞∞∞∞∞

Doc Morgan Trucking had been awarded a contract several years earlier as exclusive carrier for Atchison Industries, an arrangement benefiting both firms. Atchison was originally a farm and ranching equipment manufacturer that later branched into other fields, including lab equipment. Doc Morgan signed the original contract himself shortly before he, at the age of seventy-four, became tangled in ropes on a flatbed and suffered a fatal injury.

The trucking company was now owned by Sally Tremaine, Dix O'Donnell, Kelsey Brannigan, Vicky Lovato the office manager, and the only male member of the company, Slim Perkins, the ownership structure formalized in Doc Morgan's will.

Sally, CEO of the company, did her best to follow Doc's standards of integrity and customer service. Her once deep auburn-colored ponytail was, during the past few years, turning a silver gray.

"Let's grab a quick breakfast, Dix. Then head for the college campus." Her black cowboy hat and leather gloves rested on the panel between her seat and Dix's. She glanced at her wristwatch. "We made good time last night. They won't be expecting us until 9:00 A.M." She eased the rig into a slot close to the truck stop's front entrance and cut the engine.

"You did some good driving these past few hours, kiddo." Dix stretched her arms above her head and yawned. "Colorado Springs to Douglas, Wyoming."

"Thanks, but believe me"—she nodded toward the motel a short distance down the highway—"this old girl is looking forward to checking into that Holiday Inn for a good long shower after we make delivery." She rubbed the back of her hand across her chin and stepped down from the cab.

They eased across the brown vinyl seats of a booth in the eatery and Dix picked up the breakfast menu. She wore rimless glasses and her wavy white hair was cut short, just touching the collar of her blue denim shirt. "I'll try to raise Kelsey after we leave here. She may have been caught in that bad-ass storm last night. Hope she and Max are okay."

"Good idea." Sally set her gloves on the table. "I never worry about Kelsey and Max. Those two can take care of themselves."

"She's been on my mind this morning, though. I hope you're right."

5

KELSEY PLACED ANOTHER DOLLOP OF DOG FOOD ON THE PAPER PLATE AND slid it toward the raven. "I'm going to get you out of here somehow, Midnight. We're going to take care of that injured wing and get you healed and flying again."

The large bird made a relaxed *quork*.

Her monologue with Midnight was suddenly interrupted by a buzzing sound. Intermittent at first, then steady—coming from a few feet to the rear of the raven in the darker area beneath the church floor. The sound became louder. She saw movement and felt the hair rising on her arms.

"Oh shit, oh dear! . . . Stay back, Max. We've got ourselves a rattle-snake. Probably attracted by the smell of the dog food."

Barely visible in the early morning light, she saw the telltale black diamonds running against a light gray background along its back. It was coiled and about the same size as the raven. Midnight froze with the dog food in his beak. Kelsey held her breath. She watched the rattler flick its forked tongue up and down while the rattling continued. Max whined, his ears flat against his head.

Kelsey's cell phone rang. "Shit!" she whispered through her teeth. She remembered reading somewhere that snakes have no hearing. But ravens and dogs and people did! She rolled slowly to her side, reaching for the holster holding the small flip phone. Her fingers undid the holster latch, then grasped the phone and carried it to her ear. "Hello."

"Kelsey, this is Dix. Just checking in to see if you and Max survived that storm we heard about."

Kelsey glanced at the buzzing rattler and took a deep breath. Midnight slowly swallowed the beakful of dog food and reached for another.

"Dix," Kelsey whispered, "I'm dealing with a rattlesnake. I'll call you back."

"Oh, sweet Jesus," Dix stuttered. "Yes, call me back."

Kelsey flipped the cell phone cover closed, clutched it in her hand,

and rolled back onto her stomach. The rattler was still coiled, but the rattles had stopped. She took another deep breath and let it out slowly. The raven turned his head to her. There was no more dog food on the paper plate.

"Midnight," Kelsey whispered, "you have a big appetite." She reached for the plate and slowly drew it back for a refill when she heard the sound of horse hooves approaching from behind. The soft nicker from a horse. And a snort.

Then a man's voice. "Need any help?"

She turned her head. At eye level fifteen feet away were a pair of beat-up cowboy boots. And a handsome cowboy, mid-forties, wearing a weather-beaten cowboy hat. Six feet tall and holding a sorrel horse's reins in his right hand. Standing beside the horse was a brown and white Australian Shepherd.

She glanced back at the rattler. The rattles were silent and the coil began to relax.

Midnight squawked a subtle reminder he was still hungry.

Kelsey rolled back to her side and looked up at the cowboy. "I've got an injured raven here under the flooring," she said. "Might have a broken wing."

Max ran over to the shepherd and the two dogs engaged in their sniffing, prancing, challenging, and wagging ritual.

"Max," she said.

The dog returned to her side.

"Want me to take a look?" the cowboy asked.

"Not just yet," Kelsey murmured. Max stood motionless. She could feel his breath against her neck. "Coiled up behind the raven is a rattlesnake. Let's let him quiet down first."

Max whined. The shepherd raised its head.

The eastern sky brightened with early morning sunlight. Kelsey turned back to the raven. He looked at her and let out a *quork*. He turned his head to the snake then back to Kelsey.

"By the way, what's your name?" Kelsey asked.

"Rick Delgado. You're parked on my property." He chuckled. "And be careful, lady. Rattlesnakes have been known to kill people."

From the west came the faint wail of a diesel locomotive horn.

The rattler coiled once again, preparing to strike.

"I'm totally aware of the danger, Mr. Delgado. Pleasure to meet you. My name's Brannigan. Kelsey Brannigan. Do you own this old church?"

"Nope. My property line runs along this driveway beside it. That's my ranch house right over there." He pointed north to a house and barn with red propanel roofing.

"Can't see it from down here on my stomach, but I'm sure it's very nice."

"Let me get something to distract the rattler. Try to draw him out from under there."

"I'm a helluva lot closer to him than you are. Just what do you have in mind?"

"Stand by." He reached for a branch in the mesquite and broke it off, then stripped it with his hand. "I'll get that critter out of there so you can feed your raven." He glanced at the open can of dog food beside Kelsey's elbow and grinned.

He patted his shepherd. "Stay," he said. The dog, standing between Rick and his sorrel mare, sat and looked up awaiting his next order. Rick walked behind and around Kelsey and Max. "Keep your dog next to you. I don't want him chasing after the snake."

He dropped his large frame to the ground a short distance from Kelsey. He held the stripped tree branch and eased the end of the branch toward the rattler. The snake's rattles broke the silence and its coil tensed. His black forked tongue flashed as he struck at the branch.

Rick tapped the snake's coil and it struck the branch once again. He tapped once more. The snake instantly uncoiled and sped toward the darker area beneath the floor.

Kelsey grinned. "Good work."

"Believe me, he wants to get rid of us as much as we want to get rid of him." Rick stood. "I need to get back to work rounding up strays. That damned storm spooked the herd last night, big time." He glanced over at his dog still sitting beside the pinto. "C'mon girl." The dog ran to him. He reached down and patted her. "This is my buddy, Molly."

Kelsey stood and looked at the dog. "Molly, I think you and my Max have already met!" She looked up at Rick. "Thanks for stopping to help."

He took his gloves out of his back pocket. "Still have three strays out here someplace."

Kelsey glanced at Rick's sorrel mare. "What's your horse's name?"

He tipped his hat back. "Miss Fill."

"That's an unusual name."

"I named her after one of the greatest cow horses ever. A horse named Fillinic."

"Fillinic?"

"An unbelievable cutting horse. There's even been a song written about her."

"Was she from around here?"

"No, she was born in Arizona. Owned by a cowboy named Greg Ward. The two of them won every award and championship there was. I watched her compete a couple times. In Arizona and California. Unbelievable horse." He looked down and kicked a small rock with his boot, then nodded toward his mare. "Miss Fill is the best horse I've ever owned. That's why I named her after Fillinic."

"She's a beautiful animal." Kelsey held out her hand. "Good luck finding those strays."

He shook her hand. "What are your plans with the raven?"

She bent forward and pushed the plate with the rest of the dog food toward Midnight. "Poor creature is badly injured." She watched as Midnight picked pieces of canned dog food off the paper plate. "Probably happened during last night's storm." She glanced over at the tractor trailer. "Like you, I have work to do. Need to get back on the road. But I can't just leave this injured bird here like this. Max found him before sunrise. It was still dark." She shook her head. "I'd like to take him to a veterinarian back home in Albuquerque. Get him mended and back in the air."

"That's mighty noble." Rick scratched his chin and glanced at the big 18-wheeler. "I have an idea."

Kelsey raised her eyebrows.

"Let me see the inside of your crew cab. I might be able to whip a temporary holding pen together for you. I've got some chicken wire back in the barn."

"Really?" Her cell phone rang. She took it out and flipped it open. The caller ID read "Dix O'Donnell."

"Hello, Dix. I'm sorry I didn't call you back . . . Yes, I'm okay." She took a deep breath. "Yes, thank God the rattlesnake's gone."

"Oh, sweet Jesus, Sally and I have been worried sick about you, girl." Dix sighed. "We're just finishing breakfast here in Douglas, Wyoming. Are you really okay?"

"Douglas, Wyoming. Home of the Jackalope! Beautiful country. I love it up there! And yes, thanks to a handsome cowboy named Rick Delgado, I'm fine, Dix."

"My goodness, child," Dix laughed. "Rattlesnakes and handsome cowboys. You do know how to live!"

"I can do without the rattlesnakes, Dix." She paused. "We're about to wrap things up here and I'll be back on the road. I'll call you when I get home."

Kelsey flipped the phone cover closed and turned around. Rick Delgado was on Miss Fill at a slow gallop, heading toward his ranch barn with Molly running close behind.

6

SALLY WAS FACING THE PARKING LOT OF THE TRUCK STOP CAFÉ. AS SHE AND Dix began to get up from the table to leave, she noticed a man with an Indiana Jones hat getting out of a black Range Rover with California license plates. From the passenger side emerged a young woman wearing high heels and a mini-skirt. Sally froze. "Dix."

"What?" Dix's eyes widened as she turned to see the woman. "High heels? Up here?"

"That's Jake Brattan."

"Oh, sweet Jesus. I thought he was in prison."

As Brattan and the woman entered the dining area, Sally reached to the end of the table and picked up a menu and looked down at it. "They're walking to one of the tables in back."

"The same guy that sexually assaulted one of your employees at the ranch?"

Sally nodded. "That's the one."

"Then tried to cut our brake lines outside Durango?"

Sally watched the waitress walk to Brattan's table. "Uh-huh. That's why the bastard was locked up at Cañon City."

"What are we going to do?" Dix whispered.

"We're going to get up, walk over to the cashier and pay the bill, then we're going to walk out of here."

❦❦❦❦❦

Jake Brattan's brown hair and carefully trimmed beard were beginning to turn gray. He looked up and his eyes followed Sally and Dix as they paid for their breakfast and walked out of the café.

He'd once been one of her hands on the cattle ranch straddling the Colorado/New Mexico border. Even he would admit he wasn't the most experienced and competent cowboy around, but following a string of losses at nearby casinos, he was in need of a job and arrived at the ranch seeking work during a Rocky Mountain blizzard when Sally was desperate for another cowboy to help round up her herd.

In truth, Jake was a trust baby whose wealthy parents lived in Argentina, where he learned to ride. His father threw him out of the house when he flunked college and shipped him to the United States with the promise of monthly checks so long as he stayed there.

Jake had been on Sally's payroll for two weeks when he forced a young female employee onto the bed in a guest cabin she was cleaning. The girl's cries for help brought Sally storming into the room, where she fired him on the spot. He swore he'd get even. Tried to kill her "and her bitch friend Dix O'Donnell" one time. North of Durango. A group of leather-jacketed bikers from Montana caught him cutting their Kenworth brake lines. He served thirty-six months in Cañon City.

∽∽∽∽∽

The journey home to Argentina was made less dreaded for Jake by plentiful alcoholic beverages served in the airline's First Class section. His mother, Consuelo, met him at the Pico Truncado Airport and drove him home. Other than her speaking briefly of the embarrassment his American prison time brought to the family, few words were spoken during the drive to the family cattle ranch, Estancia Brattan, southwest of the city.

At dinner that evening, Alfonso Brattan, Jake's father, sat at the head of the dining room table. To his right, at the side of the table, sat Consuelo. Joaquin, who preferred the name Jake, sat at the other end. Alfonso's hair and moustache had turned white, but he was as physically fit as any of the gauchos on the large estancia.

They finished their meal and the servants had cleared the table when Jake stood and announced he was going to town to meet with some friends.

"You will sit down," Alfonso said in a stern voice, a voice Jake, now fifty-five years old, had not heard in thirty years.

"Excuse me."

Alfonso slammed his hand against the heavy wooden table. "Sit!"

Jake eased back down to the chair.

"And how are you going to get to town?"

"I will drive Mother's car."

"Have you asked your mother?"

"No." He turned to Consuelo. "May I use your car?"

Consuelo, her five-foot, 105-pound frame tightening, gripped the arms of her chair. "Why am I always in the middle?" She scowled at Alfonso, then turned to Jake. "I am ashamed of you, Joaquin. You are released from an American prison and you come back here expecting to be welcomed like the prodigal son." She took her napkin from her lap and tossed it on the table. "You can walk to town." She stood and left the room.

The two men stared at each other down the length of the long table.

Alfonso broke the silence. "Your mother and I were hoping one day to see you or Maria take over the ranch, Joaquin, but now . . . you are a convicted felon and an embarrassment to me and to the family. Your sister is interested only in having babies. Perhaps someday she or one of her children . . ." He grasped the sides of the table and stared outside at the cattle grazing in a distant pasture. "I do not wish for you to remain here any longer." He turned and stared at Jake. "When you return to America, which I demand that you do, I will ask the bank trustee to deposit ten thousand U.S. dollars in your bank account every month for as long as I live. After I die, your inheritance will be one hundred thousand dollars. If you ever again return to Argentina this arrangement is cancelled." He took a deep breath and let it out. "Joaquin, I want you out of here in forty-eight hours."

"I will go say goodbye to Mother and telephone my friend, Raul, to come pick me up to take me to the airport to return to the States right now." He paused. "Thank you for your financial assistance. And my inheritance." Then he stood. "Piss on you father."

"There was a time, Joaquin, that I thought you would make something of yourself. A time long past. Get out of my sight. Now!"

Several minutes later, Alfonso heard a car approach down the long driveway and stop in front of the house. The front door opened and closed, then a car door closed. He continued to stare at the cattle outside.

〰〰〰〰

Brattan walked over to the restaurant window facing the parking lot and watched as Sally and Dix got into the Kenworth and drove the short distance to their motel.

7

RICK DELGADO STOOD ON THE PASSENGER SIDE OF KELSEY'S PETERBILT with four crude wooden frames hanging from his wrist and a roll of chicken wire under his arm. Kelsey reached up and opened the door. "What I did," he said, "was grab some scrap pieces of wood lying around the barn and whip together these frames for a small four-sided cage to fit in the sleeper cab."

"Wow! That's great."

"After I wire the frames together I'll wrap this chicken wire around them and you and your raven will be in business."

"You don't know how much I appreciate your help, considering you still have stray cattle out there wandering around."

"This won't take long, but I'll need your help. Get up there in the cab and I'll hand these things to you. Together we'll get the job done."

Within minutes, Rick was kneeling on the floor of the sleeper cab, wiring the frames of the cage together while Kelsey assisted from the other side.

"What kind of mileage do you get with a truck like this?" he asked.

"About seven miles per gallon. It burns diesel."

"Yeah, I know. How much weight can you carry?"

"Fully loaded, my max is 80,000 pounds spread over eighteen wheels."

"Forty tons. That's impressive." He twisted two strands of wire together and snipped their ends. "We need to put something on the floor to rest the cage on." He looked around the small crew cab. "Like a sheet of plastic under newspapers. The raven probably isn't housebroken." He grinned.

Kelsey reached to a shelf inside the small closet. "Here's a plastic garbage bag. And"—she pulled a newspaper from beneath the microwave "a newspaper."

"Perfect." Rick tossed his hat onto the narrow cabin bed against the back wall, then spread out the plastic bag on a small floor area and spread the newspaper over it. "I've never met a lady trucker before. How long have you been driving?" He reached for the wire cutters she was holding.

"I started driving for my dad in Seattle, then spent time in the Army as a trucker before taking this job driving for Doc Morgan Trucking in Albuquerque." She held the ends of two frames together, forming a corner of the cage, while Rick wired them together. "All told, I've been driving about twelve years."

"Do you live in Albuquerque?

"I live in Corrales."

"Nice area, Corrales." Rick wrapped two wires around the frame and snipped their ends. "How many long-haul drivers are women would you guess?"

"I've read we make up about five percent." She laughed. "We're definitely a minority."

"Hand me the roll of chicken wire." He studied what was now a four-sided frame of a bird cage resting on the floor of the cab. His tousled hair came alive under the cabin's skylight. "I've been thinking of selling my place here." He nodded toward his ranch. "There's a spread over near Stanley I'm interested in."

"Where's Stanley?"

"About fifty miles east of Albuquerque. Over in your area."

"That's nice. I like living in the area."

"Is it tough being a woman driver?"

"At times. One of the biggest challenges is being a woman in a man's industry. I've learned to maintain my femininity and not try to be one of the boys."

"Makes sense." He anchored one end of the chicken wire along a corner of the frame and began rolling the wire around the other corners. "You married?"

"You sure ask a lot of questions. Are you a newspaper reporter on the side?" She smirked. "Nope, I'm not married. Came close in the Army. How about you?"

Rick shook his head. "I guess I do ask a lot of questions, huh?" He grunted and tugged on the wire. "I'm divorced."

"I'm sorry."

"It's just Molly and Fill and me now." He looked across at her. "We're almost finished with this job. Hand me the pliers."

She picked up the pliers from the floor and gave them to him. His fingers brushed against the back of her hand. She felt her face flush.

Rick twisted two strands of wire together and leaned back. "Mission accomplished! You and I just built a four-sided bird cage with an open top." He reached for his hat, then looked at his watch. "Twenty minutes. Not bad for a couple of amateurs."

"You are unbelievable!" Kelsey examined the cage and reached across to take Rick's hand. "Thank you."

"You ever thought about living on a ranch?"

Caught off guard, she hesitated for an instant. "Can't say that I have."

"It's not a bad life." He winked at her and gathered his tools, then stepped down into the cab. "I'm going to have to leave it up to you to get the raven in here by yourself." He slid across the passenger seat and dropped to the ground. "I'd like to help you out, but I've got some lost cattle to find."

She stepped to the ground. "I understand. Totally. Thank you." She glanced down at Max and Molly standing beside each other. "The dogs seem to have become friends." She smiled. "I hope our paths cross again."

Rick flashed a shy grin. "I hope so too. If you have a pen and a piece of paper I'd like to write down my address and phone number. If you're ever by here again." He raised his eyebrows. "Maybe you could give me your address and phone number, too."

"My only phone is my cell phone." She reached back and opened the passenger side door of the rig to retrieve a notepad and pen.

"Me too." He patted the phone holster on his belt.

They exchanged phone numbers and Kelsey placed the piece of paper with Rick's number into a shirt pocket.

"Keep me posted on that raven." He smiled and tipped his hat.

"I will."

Rick walked to Miss Fill. "Take care of yourself, Kelsey." He slipped his boot into the left stirrup and swung into the saddle. Miss Fill took off at a trot with Molly running alongside.

Kelsey watched him ride away. "You take care of yourself as well, cowboy," she whispered as she turned toward the church.

Midnight was right where she left him, resting on the piece of wood beneath the church's failing floor. The paper plate had no trace of dog food. He had eaten it all. She got down on her stomach once again, holding a small pan of clear fresh water. Max stood beside her, watching.

She placed the pan of water on the end of the narrow wood panel and eased it forward. Midnight didn't flinch or show any concern as the pan came close to touching his beak and stopped. He stretched forward and took a sip. Then he turned to Kelsey and she would later swear he winked at her. She glanced skyward. Four hours had passed since she and the bird first met.

She began moving toward him, inch by inch, maintaining eye contact—cautiously closing the distance between them. She reached forward with her fingertips almost touching the tip of his beak. Then she paused. Her arm and neck muscles were tiring. Midnight turned his beak to examine her gloved hand. He pecked at her fingers, almost playfully. Then he took another sip of water and turned his head to study her face.

Kelsey wanted to wrap both of her hands around Midnight and lift him from his temporary shelter, but realized she couldn't from flat on her stomach. She withdrew her hand slowly and shifted to a kneeling position. Midnight followed her movements. She took a deep breath and exhaled, then inched back toward the bird on her knees, moving cautiously across the tarp. She leaned forward on her hands, now three or four inches from Midnight. He studied one of her hands. Then the other. Then he looked up at her. She eased her left hand against his side closest to her and wrapped her right hand around the other side. He flinched. Then he relaxed.

Max turned his head to the side with a barely audible whine.

Kelsey lifted the bird slowly. He extended his long Ichabod Crane legs but didn't resist her hold. He was midair, free of his resting spot. She brought him slowly to her chest, holding him against her jacket with her right hand. She pressed against the ground with her left hand and rose slowly to a standing position. "Good boy, Midnight. Good boy," she whispered.

The bird made a half-hearted attempt to free himself, then turned his head and looked ahead as Kelsey walked the short distance to the truck. Max followed at her heels.

8

"THERE'S ONE PLACE IN WYOMING I'VE ALWAYS WANTED TO SEE." DIX WAS spinning a few strands of spaghetti around her fork at a restaurant near the Wyoming State Fair Grounds.

"Where's that," Sally asked, almost fully rested after a three-hour nap. She set her fork on her plate. "This is a big state with a lot to see."

Dix swallowed the spaghetti and took a sip of red wine. "Devils Tower. I've heard about it and read about it." She spun some more spaghetti. "And there was that marvelous movie with Richard Dreyfuss."

"*Close Encounters?*"

"Yes." Dix lit up. "*Close Encounters of the Third Kind!* I loved the theme music. I can hear those pipes playing right now!"

"Dah-dah-dah-dah-dah," Sally chimed in.

"That's it!" Dix laughed. "How far are we from Devils Tower?"

"It's up in the northeast corner of the state. As a matter of fact, I'd like to see it too. Let's pull out the map when we get back to the room."

"I'll call our broker to see if we can find a load to take up that way. No sense deadheading that distance with an empty trailer."

They drove north on Highway 59 with the trailer almost filled with supplies and merchandise for the Devils Tower Trading Post and two other businesses in the vicinity. They crested the top of a mountain pass and headed down the backside when a sudden gust of wind slammed against the side of the rig.

"Holy crap!" Dix shouted. "Where the hell did that come from?"

"We've been hearing about Wyoming and its mountain winds. Guess we should have expected that."

Dix shifted to a lower gear. "Forewarned is forearmed, as they say." She bit her lower lip. "This old girl will be more attentive from now on."

"Old-time Wyoming truckers have their favorite stretches of terror. Dead Horse Bend and Beaver Rim, to name a couple."

"My favorite story is the one we heard at that truck stop in Provo a couple of years ago."

"About the trucker from Lander, Wyoming?" Sally shook her head. "He and his rig hit by unbelievable crosswinds got blown over flat on his side—two times within sixty days!"

"Real butt-puckerers," Dix chortled.

Between Gillette and Moorcroft, forty miles from Devils Tower, acrid smoke began pouring from the air vents into the cab. Dix was still driving.

"What the hell!" she shouted, immediately downshifting and braking to the right shoulder of the highway.

"Good God Almighty!" Sally lowered the window on the passenger side and reached to the side panel for a fire extinguisher. As soon as Dix brought the rig to a stop and cut the engine, Sally jumped to the ground and spun to the front side of the engine hood and raised it. Flames leapt toward her as she frantically sprayed the chemical retardant into the flames from side to side. She was barely aware of Dix jumping from her side of the cab with another fire extinguisher.

Brakes squealed and engines quieted as other vehicles slowed down to gawk at the smoking inferno and the two women extinguishing the flames.

〰〰〰〰

Among the gawkers slowing to rubberneck was the driver of a black Range Rover with California license plates. Jake Brattan's cold brown eyes surveyed the scene of the two women with their fire extinguishers. The left pocket of his work shirt was torn with part of the shirt label missing. He grinned. "Squirm, Sally Tremaine, you bitch. Enjoy standing there peeing in your pants." He tipped his Indiana Jones hat. "We'll meet again. Somewhere. Sometime." Beside him sat the mini-skirted woman. She was smoking a joint and running her hand up and down his leg.

〰〰〰〰

An 18-wheeler broke free from the gawkers, shot to the side of the inter-state, and came to a cloud-of-dust stop fifty yards ahead of them.

The husky young trucker jumped out, unhitched a heavy-duty extinguisher from the side of the rig, and dashed toward Sally and Dix. "Get back! Both of you!" he shouted.

They jumped out of the way as the linebacker of a man rushed up and stood beside the Kenworth's engine, smothering the fire with the fire extinguisher.

In a short period of time, the last flame flickered out and the bitter stench weakened in the high Rockies wind. He climbed up to take a close look at the large Caterpillar engine.

Sally and Dix stepped forward behind him.

"You may have saved our lives," Dix said.

"Had no choice," he grunted. Sweat dripped from his face. "You ladies were in a bad place."

Sally rested her gloved hand on the fender. "Can you tell what caused the fire?"

"Dunno." He ran his fingers around the turbo air pressure unit on the passenger side of the engine and stopped. "Think I found it."

Sally eased closer as the trucker reached into his pocket and pulled out a utility rag and wiped a section of the unit. He inched closer and examined it. "Somebody loosened the air pressure nut."

"What!" Sally said.

"Only enough to allow oil to spray back on the turbo and the exhaust manifold." He glanced down at Sally. "After several miles, bingo, you've got an engine fire."

"My God!"

"They knew what they were doing. Didn't want it to ignite too soon. They wanted a delayed fire—after you'd been on the road awhile."

"Oh, sweet Jesus." Dix placed her hands on her cheeks.

The trucker eased back down to the ground and turned to them. By this time several bystanders were gathered around the tractor trailer. The women ignored them.

"Is there anyone out to get either of you?" he asked.

Sally looked at him and nodded.

"I'd be careful, ma'am. It's none of my business, but I'd be careful."

"We're both very grateful to you." Sally held out her hand. "This is Dix O'Donnell. I'm Sally Tremaine."

"Bill. Bill Faucett." He shook hands with Sally, then Dix. "Pleased to know you." He wiped his forehead with the utility rag. "I tightened the nut. You'll be okay 'til you get back home. Have your mechanic check it out while he's cleaning the engine."

"Bill Faucett, there's a special place in heaven for you," Sally said.

"Oh, I don't know about that." He smiled. "By the way"—he reached into a shirt pocket—"I found this piece of cloth stuck on a screw head." He handed her a ragged piece of black fabric with a *Dickies/Sears* label. "Might have torn off someone's shirt."

Sally took the fabric and turned it over in her hand.

From a distance came the wail of a siren.

"Are you gonna report this incident to the cops?" Bill asked.

Sally glanced around at the onlookers. Most were leaving the scene. "I don't think so," she said. "I have suspicions, but no evidence." She held up the black fabric. "Other than this."

"I understand." He nodded. "Good luck, you two. Glad I could help." He turned and walked back to his tractor trailer.

They were silent as they watched him leave. Dix said softly, "He's a good man."

"Indeed, he is," Sally replied. "Want me to drive, kiddo?"

"No, I'm fine."

A Wyoming Highway patrolman drove up with lights flashing.

The two women walked around the rig searching for other signs of tampering.

"You ladies need any help?" the patrolman asked as he approached.

"No." Sally glanced at the blackened engine hood, then back at the patrolman. "We had a problem, but with the help of that trucker who just pulled out, we're okay now. Thanks."

After a few pleasantries, the patrolman left. Sally and Dix walked to the Kenworth and strapped in. Sally placed the piece of torn fabric in the glove box.

"The smoke's cleared the engine and the cab," Dix said. She glanced at

Sally. "I think we know who may have sabotaged the truck back in Douglas."

Sally nodded. "I think we do. That son of a bitch. I'm going to start packing the Smith & Wesson in my right ankle holster. I have concealed weapon permits for New Mexico and Colorado."

"What about Wyoming?" Dix started the engine.

"Wyoming is one of eight states which allow individuals to carry concealed weapons without a permit."

"It would make me feel better if you started carrying it, Sally." She pulled back onto the highway.

They drove northeast on Highway 14, then north on State Road 24 and watched Devils Tower come into view. They turned silent as the distance closed and the Tower grew larger.

"Isn't that the most beautiful sight you've ever seen in your life?" Dix asked.

"Takes my breath away."

9

KELSEY STOOD BETWEEN THE TRUCK AND THE OLD CHURCH AND GAZED across the open field to Rick's ranch house, hoping he might be outside so she could wave goodbye. There was no sign of him. She lifted Max into the cab then climbed in and started the engine. Just for the fun of it she reached up and pulled the air horn lanyard for a quick blast.

She eased down the dirt road beside the old church with Max standing on the passenger seat and Midnight resting on the floor of his temporary chicken wire quarters. She turned right on Highway 84 to Fort Sumner and drove past the Billy the Kid Museum and gravesite.

North of Fort Sumner, she phoned ahead to the Santa Rosa drop-off point, alerting them to her estimated delivery time of the wooden pallets from Clovis. A crew was standing by when she arrived and she, Max, and Midnight were soon on Interstate 40 heading to Albuquerque.

Midnight was traveling surprisingly well. His injured right wing continued to hang limply at his side, but he nibbled at remnants of the canned dog food and sounded an occasional *quark*. He did a lot of looking around at his new surroundings in the sleeper cab with its strange sounds. Max left the passenger seat from time to time to sniff and check on his new traveling companion.

After they drove through Billboard Alley between Santa Rosa and Clines Corners, Kelsey contacted Vicky Lovato at home base in Albuquerque.

"Vicky, I need your help with something."

"Whatever it is I'm eager to do it!" Vicky laughed. "Before Sally and Dix left for Wyoming, Sally handed me a fistful of regulatory reports to file with the state and the feds. I'm ready for a break! What do you need?"

Kelsey had been impressed by Vicky from the moment they met. Her wit, her loyalty to the memory of Doc Morgan, and her work ethic. She was a member of the Kewa Pueblo tribe located between Albuquerque and Santa Fe, and had long, almost luminescent black hair and a playful sense of humor. Her father was a former Marine, her mother an active medical laboratory technician. Vicky had been Doc Morgan's secretary during his last years as a practicing internist and before that was one of his patients. She followed him to his trucking company and his lifelong dream to be a big rig trucker.

"I need for you to call Dr. Kate Harrison's office," Kelsey said. "She's Max's veterinarian."

"Is something wrong with Max?"

"No, Max is fine. We found an injured raven in Taiban, over near Fort Sumner. I've got the raven in the truck. I need to find out if Dr. Harrison treats birds. If not, can she recommend another vet."

"What? Kelsey, are you serious?"

"I'll explain the details when I get to the office."

"You *are* serious. I'll call you back in fifteen minutes."

Midnight jumped at the strange sound of Kelsey's cell phone ring. "Kelsey," Vicky said, "I spoke with Dr. Harrison. Yes, she cares for birds and she wants to see the raven. She may refer you to some wildlife people, though. We made an appointment for two o'clock this afternoon. Can you make it?"

"Vicky, you are a godsend. You bet I can." She glanced at the center rearview mirror and saw Midnight resting quietly.

"She has that big parking lot for horse trailers, so you'll be able to pull the Peterbilt almost to the front door."

"You're an angel."

Vicky laughed. "I can think of a few people who might disagree with that."

"Would you mind calling her office again to tell them I have the raven in the truck in a crude chicken wire enclosure? I'll need someone from the clinic to come out to help transport him inside."

"Will do, Bronco Brannigan. Drive carefully. Ten-four."

The veterinary assistant, Paco Sanchez, a young Hispanic with a weight lifter's physique, placed Midnight in a large bird cage he brought out to the truck from the clinic. He covered the cage with a towel and carried it, holding Midnight, into the clinic, proceeded down the hallway to the examining room, and set it carefully on the exam table. Then he and Kelsey waited for Dr. Harrison, who was with another patient.

She arrived within minutes with a warm smile and a firm handshake. "So, tell me about the raven, Kelsey." She placed her hands in the large pockets of her dark blue lab coat.

Kelsey stood on the other side of the examination table beside Paco. "Max and I pulled off the highway in a small village near Fort Sumner last evening during a nightmare rainstorm. It was almost a tornado. Place called Taiban."

"I'm familiar with the area. And I heard the weather report on the news last night. There was, in fact, a small tornado. Good thing you pulled off the highway."

"We rode it out." She looked down at Midnight. "Unfortunately, this fella wasn't as lucky. Early this morning I let Max out of the rig to make his rounds. He'd been out just a few minutes when he began barking to get my attention. I got out of the truck and walked over to where he was standing beside an old abandoned Presbyterian church. He was looking down beneath the dilapidated flooring of the church. There sat this dear bird. I think he got slammed in the storm and injured his wing. I've fed him some canned dog food and he's had some water."

"How did you get him in the truck?"

"A very kind cowboy happened by on his horse and helped me get the raven into the truck. Then he rigged a temporary pen with some chicken wire."

"God bless kind cowboys." Dr. Harrison smiled. "You did all the right things. Let's take a look at the patient."

She bent over the table and looked into the cage. "Hello there, Mr. Raven," she said softly. "I'm going to put my hands inside the cage to touch you very gently." She unlatched two side doors and slowly moved her fingers to the sides of the bird. He flinched when she touched his right wing. "Broken wings are a common injury. Birds' bones are pretty fragile." She eased her hands back from the cage. "Paco, I'm going to need an x-ray."

"Yes, ma'am."

"Prepare an anesthetic."

"Will do."

Kelsey took a step back from the stainless-steel examination table.

"Kelsey," Dr. Harrison said, "I'd like you to remain here beside me. The raven knows you and this procedure will be stressful for him."

"Certainly."

"What are your plans for the bird?"

"To take him home, nurse him back to health, and set him free."

She smiled. "A very kind objective. I wish it were that easy."

"What do you mean?"

"Ravens are a protected species. You would need a federal permit and a state permit to take him home and rehabilitate him yourself. To even apply for a permit, you need to have at least 100 hours hands-on experience. It's pretty rigorous."

"Wow."

"I'll telephone a friend at the Wildlife Rescue office as soon as I have a few minutes. She can provide us with the guidance we need."

"Isoflurane?" Paco interrupted.

"Yes," Dr. Harrison turned back to Kelsey. "This won't be an injection. We'll be using inhalant gas. Also, because a sedated bird can lose a lot of body heat, we'll cover him from the neck down with a towel. He'll be on his back with his right wing spread out and held in place with veterinarian bandaging tape which won't stick to his feathers."

Kelsey nodded and returned her attention to Midnight. She bent down. "Be brave, Midnight. You're going to be okay, boy."

The raven looked at her and cocked his head.

Dr. Harrison observed the exchange. "Kelsey, Paco and I may try to hire you." Her eyes softened. "You have that rare gift of knowing how to communicate with feathered and furry creatures."

Kelsey grinned. "That's a big ten-four! I'd enjoy working with you and Paco, but I belong in my 18-wheeler."

"Ten-four yourself! I love you truckers! I used to have a CB radio in my car and I listened to you guys chattering back and forth with each other. That was several years ago when I was doing a lot of house calls at farms and cattle ranches."

"Do you still get out?"

She sighed. "Not as much as I used to. I miss it. C.W. McCall was my hero."

"Mine, too. He and his rubber duck."

"I still have his CDs stashed in my car."

Just as the x-ray procedure concluded, Dr. Harrison was called away to another emergency. "Paco, you and Kelsey keep an eye on our patient. I'll be back."

Kelsey and Paco stood on either side of the table engaged in light conversation while monitoring Midnight's status. The raven began to stir just as the doctor returned.

"There's no evidence of bone fracture in Midnight's wing," she said. "I'm certain, however, that there's been muscle and tendon damage. He obviously got thrown around during that storm." She reached down and removed the tape holding Midnight's wing out to his side and carefully picked him up. "What I'm going to do is fold his injured wing against his side and wrap bandaging tape around his body and beneath his left wing."

She nodded to Paco, who cut a twelve-inch strip of veterinarian bandaging tape. Together they wrapped Midnight, immobilizing his right wing.

"I telephoned my friend Roberta at the Wildlife Rescue office a few minutes ago. They and their volunteers rehabilitate injured wildlife animals and birds like Midnight, and guide them through the healing process to recovery. They then release them back to the wild."

Kelsey glanced down at Midnight, then up at Dr. Harrison. "Could I be involved somehow? I feel a definite attachment to this guy."

Dr. Harrison patted Kelsey's arm. "I'm certain you could. From my experience with the rescue folks, you'd be invited to visit Midnight as often as you wish. The volunteers and staff have spent years doing this sort of thing. You and I have not. They're equipped with knowledge and experience that'll better assure Midnight's recovery and return to the wild. Your visits and being a part of the process could be a real plus."

Kelsey nodded. "Thank you."

"One of their volunteers will drop by as soon as I call them. I wanted to have these few minutes with you first."

"I understand. I just want to help this guy get back in the air."

"Place him on the floor, Paco," Dr. Harrison said. "Let's see if he can walk and breathe okay and move his left wing."

Midnight stood, somewhat wobbly. His movement was restricted by the tape, and the anesthesia had not yet worn off. He pooped. Then he waddled toward the door. Kelsey got down on the floor to block his path. He stopped and fixed his eyes on her. Sounds of people and other pets began echoing down the hallway on the other side of the doorway. He turned around and waddled in the other direction.

Dr. Harrison bent down and picked him up. "I think he's going to recover fairly quickly."

"That's wonderful."

"I don't think he'd have made it if you and Max hadn't come along." She paused. "I've seen signs of bonding between you and Midnight. After he heals and is released, he may find his way back to Taiban or he might decide to stick around this area. Or perhaps he'll choose to adopt you and Max." She smiled.

Kelsey felt Kate's words and took a deep breath. "That would be so cool." She glanced down at Midnight resting on the examination table.

Kate wrapped a towel around him and handed him to Kelsey. "I'll telephone Roberta now. She'll send someone over from the Wildlife Rescue office."

10

"IT LOOKS LIKE A HUMONGOUS TREE STUMP WITH FLUTED SIDES," Dix said as they approached Devils Tower from the south. They'd just finished unloading cargo at the Trading Post. A color brochure describing the tower poked out of her shirt pocket.

"Such massive symmetry. Just look at it," Sally said. "Our first national monument. Teddy Roosevelt. 1906. I understand several Native American tribes are asking that its name be returned to its original Bear Lodge. It's a very sacred place to them."

"I hope their wish is granted. Indian legend has it that what you called fluted sides of the tower are actually claw marks from a giant bear."

"This brochure mentions a trail around the tower. Takes about an hour to walk."

"I think we should do it, Dix!"

"Speaking of bears, remember the surprise gift we got for Slim after we passed the Commercial Driving License test?"

"Big Brown Teddy Bear!" Sally laughed. "We found him in that toy store on the Plaza."

"Slim still straps him in the passenger seat from time to time. That bear is huge!"

"He loves it."

"Alexis, his sweet wife, thinks it's a hoot!"

They purchased tickets to join a small group to walk the trail with a park ranger and were seated on one of the park benches when Dix nudged Sally. She tilted her head to their left where, several yards away, a man in an Indiana Jones hat stood leaning against one of the ponderosa pine trees. Fear gripped her eyes. "Sally, there's Jake. Let's get out of here."

Sally turned and studied the man. Same height and weight as Jake Brattan. His back was turned toward them and he was by himself. "No one is going to determine whether or not you and I take a walk around this tower, Dix." She placed her hand on her knee. "Or anything else." Her jaw tightened. "That son of a bitch."

The man turned around and walked in their direction. They both exhaled. He wasn't Jake Brattan. As he drew closer he smiled. Then he stopped. "You ladies from around here?" He had a wide, welcoming smile, a ruddy complexion, light brown hair. There was a kindness about him. Beneath his chin, a Roman collar.

Sally relaxed. "No, Padre. We're truckers from New Mexico." She extended her hand. "My name is Sally and this is Dix."

The priest took her hand. "Lady truckers from New Mexico. My, my. Welcome to Wyoming. I'm Patrick Smith. Folks call me Father Pat. My parish, St. Matthew's, is in Gillette, southwest of here."

"Hi, Father Pat." Dix held out her hand. "We thought you might have been someone else." She smiled. "We're glad it's you."

"I'm glad it's me as well," he chuckled.

"We just made a delivery to the Trading Post and had to see Devils Tower before heading back home," Sally said.

"I'm happy that you did. This is a very spiritual place. I come up here every so often to breathe the fresh air and just walk around the tower." A slight breeze drifted through the grass beside them.

"We're looking forward to the walk," Dix said, gazing around at the forest. "I notice pieces of fabric and small bundles of cloth attached to some of the trees. What are they all about?"

Father Pat turned and looked at the cluster of ponderosa pine nearby. "Those are prayer cloths left by Indian tribal members who visit the area. The tribes gather mostly in June and the early summer months. The prayer cloths manifest their spiritual connection with the Tower. You'll notice there are also bundles of cloth attached to some of the trees. We're asked not to touch or photograph any of them. A few of the tribal members are friends of mine. Very dear friends." He held his hands behind his back. "I respect and honor their beliefs. As they respect mine." He gazed up at the majestic Tower and, surrounding it, a crystalline blue sky.

He turned back to them. "Well, I must be going." He took off his hat and shook their hands. "God bless you both."

"Thank you, Padre," Sally said.

"God bless *you*, Father Pat." Dix nodded, almost solemnly.

The priest took a few steps and stopped. He reached into his pocket and pulled out what appeared to be a couple of coins. He turned them over in his hand. "I usually carry one or two of these with me."

"What are they?" Sally asked.

"Saint Christopher medals. Saint Chris is the patron saint of travelers. He looks out for us during our life's journey, if you will. Chris has assured my safe travels throughout this region for many, many years. From time to time I meet travelers such as yourselves. I know we've not met before, but there's something about both of you that makes me think we have." He smiled and handed one of the medals to each of them. A small hole had been drilled at the top of each coin. "I would like for you to have these, to place somewhere on your person, a key ring perhaps, or in your truck so he may keep the two of you safe on the road." He paused, looking to the ground as if he was in prayer. Then he raised his eyes and winked at them. "Godspeed."

Sally and Dix stood in silence as Father Pat walked away until Dix said, almost in a whisper, "There's something about that man, Sally. I can't describe it or define it, but I feel so at peace right now."

Sally reached for her hand.

"Do I make sense?"

"More than you know."

"Are you thinking of Mike?" Dix gently squeezed her hand.

Within a few minutes, they joined the small group of sightseers, walking behind and beside the Park Service ranger and listening to her delightfully memorized presentation of the Tower's historical, geological, and cultural past.

Sally held the Saint Christopher medal in the palm of her hand throughout the tour. She was not a religious person, but somehow she felt a spiritual connection to the place and to the small piece of metal given to her by the Catholic priest. It would go on her key ring, not to be lost or misplaced, as had happened with a medal given her years previously by Father John Shannon, Mike Shannon's son.

Before she and Dix became truckers, Sally and Mike Shannon had been engaged to marry. Mike was a widower with three grown children, two sons and a daughter. He lived in Los Angeles where he was vice president of sales for a major life insurance company. He also partnered with a family member, Elena Cordova, in the ownership of a cattle ranch on the Colorado/New Mexico border, an interest that would later become Sally's.

Sally had been a senior executive with Fallbrook Companies St. Louis, where she and Mike met during a business conference. Several months later they made plans to marry. Fate had other plans. Days shy of their marriage ceremony, Mike suffered a fatal heart attack.

Engraved in Sally's mind was the image of Father John saying the funeral Mass in Pasadena. Seated beside her was Mike's daughter, Liz. Mike's other son, Buck, an Air Force pilot, was unable to be with them because of a flying assignment.

Father John's concluding remarks at the end of the Mass were interrupted by the thundering roar of an Air Force jet making a treetop-level pass over the church. It was Buck on his "flying assignment," making his final salute to his dad. She would never forget it.

Father John had given Sally a St. Christopher medal that day, which somehow became lost during one of her moves. The St. Chris given her by Father Pat would go on her key ring.

A subsequent relationship Sally had with a high school flame rekindled but soon went out. She turned her focus and energy to Doc Morgan Trucking with occasional stints behind the wheel of the robin's egg-blue Kenworth.

When the tour of Devils Tower concluded, Sally and Dix drove a short distance to Sundance, Wyoming, to spend the night. The next morning, they picked up a shipment in Moorpark for delivery in Albuquerque.

11

THE VILLAGE OF CORRALES, THE SPANISH WORD FOR *CORRALS*, LIES NORTH-west of downtown Albuquerque. Corrales and its surrounding farm-lands have been home through the centuries to Pueblo Indians, Spaniards, and Anglo settlers. Bordered by metropolitan neighbors Albuquerque and Rio Rancho, the village prides itself in maintaining its rural, agricultural way of life and slower pace of an earlier time.

Kelsey and Max had left home before daylight to deliver a ship-ment from Atchison Industries to the New Mexico State University in Las Cruces. Returning in the early evening, she left the rig in the company parking lot and continued home in the pickup. After she parked in the driveway and turned off the engine, Max jumped out and she closed the truck door, then stood and observed two ravens circling overhead.

She was pleased to find a message from Wildlife Rescue on her phone that one of their volunteers had been assigned to Midnight's reha-bilitation. His name was John Buscaglia and he lived but a short distance from her home. She hoped John Buscaglia would consent to her visiting Midnight during his rehab.

Certified by both state and federal wildlife agencies, John, twenty to twenty-five years Kelsey's senior, had been a volunteer with Wildlife Rescue for two decades. "I learned the ropes during my first volunteer years when I was assigned to assist an old-timer living further downriver near the Rio Grande Bosque," he told her during their first meeting at his home. "I was teaching fulltime at University of New Mexico in those days, so I worked only weekends as a wildlife volunteer. Damn near *every* weekend. I loved it."

They stood beside a table in one of several mews in the backyard of his four-acre property.

John had picked up Midnight at the Wildlife Rescue office the previous day and brought him home where he weighed the bird and gave him a thorough exam. Even though Dr. Harrison had conducted a physical exam, John always insisted on conducting his own examinations of all wildlife placed in his care.

Midnight sat on the table in the mew closest to John's kitchen door. The bandaging tape Dr. Harrison had prescribed was still wrapped around his body. "I'll keep the tape in place another week or so and keep it clean. The doc made the right call in keeping the injured wing immobile for several days."

In addition to the table where Midnight stood, John had constructed a ramp from the floor below plus three perches at different heights above the table.

"Ravens are frequent wintertime visitors to the cottonwood trees in the area and along the Rio Grande. During spring and early summer a majority of them fly north to the cooler mountain areas near Santa Fe, Española, and Taos."

Most of the mews were occupied by corvids (ravens, crows) and raptors (hawks, eagles, buzzards), which were at various stages of recovery from injuries or being rehabilitated for release back to the wild. The remaining mews were unoccupied, but would not be for long.

"Springtime and nesting will soon arrive along the Rio Grande," John said. "And some of the nestlings will die from human kindness."

Kelsey frowned. "What do you mean?"

"They're bumped out of a crowded nest or they get up on the edge of the nest to flap their tiny wings. Guess what? They fall to the ground! Left alone, mama bird or papa bird might manage to get them back in the nest. A man or a woman walks by, however, looks down on the ground and sees the baby bird and takes it home to save its life or takes it to the animal shelter."

"And?"

"And I'm called to pick up the bird, to bring it home and tube feed it. And hopefully save the little guy's life. Also, I have a vet that I work closely with. After I receive a bird and give it a thorough exam, I'll call the vet and drop by his office with the bird so he can check him over.

This wasn't necessary with Midnight because you'd already taken care of that with Dr. Harrison."

"Makes sense."

"If it's possible to rehab the bird, we'll do so. But if a wing is broken too badly or if we're not confident the bird will be able to survive, then we'll euthanize. That's a hard decision to make because if you try to save the bird and you succeed—and find it isn't releasable, you have to find a home for it. Or perhaps you can have it become an educational bird to take to schools or lectures or symposiums."

"There's much more to the world of wildlife rescue than I'd realized."

"I could write a book about it. Wildlife Rescue releases around a third of the feathered and furry creatures we take in."

"You're all due a lot of credit."

"I wish we were releasing a hundred percent, but that won't happen." He took a breath. "Regarding educational birds, red-tailed hawks and great horned owls are very common, as are ravens and crows. Ravens and crows, members of the corvid family, are always popular. When we go to shows or schools and we take a corvid, everybody has a story. *My grandfather had a crow and he talked like crazy.' 'I had a raven when I was a kid.'* You get all these stories. It's amazing. And it's fun."

"I'll bet it is."

"People seem to gravitate more to ravens and crows than they do to hawks or owls. They have the intelligence of dolphins. Extremely intelligent birds with keener vision than any other wild animal I've known." He grinned. "And they can be mischievous critters. You've got to keep your eyes on them. And—surprise, surprise—they poop. A lot."

Kelsey laughed. "Not good house pets."

"Hell, no!" He shook his head. "But, speaking of birds and their intelligence, I read a piece in the paper recently about Sam Shepard, the actor and playwright."

"I loved that man. He was my hero."

"And he loved New Mexico. He told a story about watching a crow up in Santa Fe one time. The crow kept diving at this red-tailed hawk again and again, just to harass him. Well, Mister Hawk finally got fed up with the damned crow and started climbing to higher altitudes. The crow couldn't keep up and quit in exhaustion. 'Outfly them,' Sam Shepard said. 'Outfly them.' That was one of his mottos."

Kelsey glanced down at Midnight standing beside his watering dish. He took a sip of water, cocked his head toward her, and uttered a *quark*. "Will Midnight be okay, John?"

"Midnight is a strong bird, with a lot of spunk. He definitely got beat up in that rainstorm."

"He looked like a drowned rat when Max and I found him beneath that church."

"You may have saved his life." John glanced at the bird. "I think we'll be releasing him in two or three weeks."

"Is he eating?"

John laughed. "Like it's the Last Supper! He wolfs his food. Particularly figs, tomatoes, and strawberries. He also lets me know he doesn't like oranges or apples. Pushes them aside with his bill and ignores them. When he's given food he likes, he sometimes thanks me with a short, soft two-note call."

"That's unreal!"

"He also likes hard-boiled eggs. I always keep a few in reserve."

"I think he's going to refuse release and take up permanent residence right here."

"I'll try not to keep him too long. Don't want him losing his hunting skills. Roadkill remains king. I keep a shovel and a bucket in the back of the pickup. Never know when you might come across a few morsels of rabbit or skunk or squirrel. I may be asking you for help in that department."

Kelsey grinned. "Just give me the word, John. Just give me the word."

⁓⁓⁓⁓⁓

Sally and Dix pulled into the company parking lot on their return from Colorado and Wyoming. They parked the Kenworth and went inside to get caught up by Vicky on office issues and the status of Kelsey and her injured raven.

The first thing Vicky did was hand Sally a stack of papers to be reviewed and letters to be signed. "Welcome back, boss."

"You've been busy, haven't you?" Sally put on her reading glasses and glanced at some of the papers. "I'll take these with me and bring them back to you tomorrow."

"Works for me."

"I'd like to drop by Kelsey's on our way home—to check on her and her big bird. I think Dix would, too, but we're whipped." She noticed Dix waiting near the office door and took a deep breath. She exhaled through puffed cheeks. "We'll go see them in a few days."

"Actually, Kelsey doesn't have the raven at her home. It's being cared for by someone from Wildlife Rescue. I think Kelsey is helping, though."

"Sounds good." Sally picked up her Stetson from a side chair and put it on. "We had an unpleasant incident up in Wyoming." Sally said. "In Douglas."

Vicky furrowed her brow.

"I'll tell you about it later. Thanks for taking care of things while we were gone."

Sally glanced up at the scheduling board for a few moments and noted there were no long hauls for Atchison. The only listed runs were local pickups and deliveries within a two-hundred-mile radius, runs easily handled by Sally and Dix commuting from their homes in Santa Fe and by Kelsey within easy reach in Corrales. Slim Perkins was available on short notice for any longer runs throughout the Rocky Mountain, Midwest, and southwest regions.

"What would we do without Slim," she asked, "strong, dependable, smiling Slim."

"We'd be hurting, boss."

Sally gave Vicky a hug. Then she and Dix got in Sally's pickup and headed to their homes in Santa Fe, sixty miles north.

12

JAKE BRATTAN'S THIRTY-SIX MONTHS IN THE COLORADO STATE PENITENTIARY did nothing to rehabilitate him. What got him there was severing the brake service line of Sally and Dix's Kenworth with a switchblade on Highway 550 between Durango and Ouray, Colorado. Plain and simple— an act of revenge. He was charged with attempted murder and aggravated assault. Until he surfaced in Douglas, Wyoming, Sally and Dix thought they had seen the last of Jake Brattan. But the nightmare was reborn.

Thanks to the bankroll supplied by his father, a fast-talking lawyer, and a bourbon-thirsty judge, the attempted murder charge was dropped. Thirty-six months in confinement was all that he served for a reduced charge of aggravated assault.

Following his release, Jake spent the brief visit with his parents in Argentina before getting crosswise with his father who, once again, tossed him out of the house, with the promise to provide him monthly income if he remained in the United States. With the monthly stipend from his father's trust his financial worries were, therefore, few. His ruggedly hand- some looks, beguiling charm, and prison background opened doors to several off-the-radar business opportunities. Among them was a position with *Brothel Row* in Pahrump, Nevada, where he became a "facilitator." His job was to identify, interview, and hire female escorts whom he would then personally "deliver" to select clients in Nevada and other neighboring western states.

Predator, manipulator, and a scoundrel, Jake was now also a pimp. And he was dangerous; released from prison he was more bilious to soci- ety than when he entered.

Sally Tremaine, a stern and disciplined woman, represented to Jake everything that he loathed. She had unintentionally erred in giving him a break. She gave him a job when he needed one. Then, in his twisted mind, she humiliated him by firing him.

Now, Jake opined, having made contact once again with his nemesis, it might be time to seek escorts for new clientele on her home turf, Santa Fe. The town, a gathering spot for movie types, tourists, and politicians, had money. It had fancy hotels. While his escorts worked, he too would work—tracking and stalking Sally Tremaine.

⬳⬳⬳⬳⬳

Since their return from Wyoming, Sally had been deskbound in the Doc Morgan office, analyzing shipping, financial, and maintenance reports with Vicky and reviewing regulatory documents. "I often wonder how many of these damned transportation experts have actually driven a rig!" she exclaimed. Vicky brought her a coffee refill.

Near the end of a busy workday, she checked the scheduling board and saw Slim was making an extended run to Little Rock while Dix and Kelsey made the one- and two-day pickups in and around Albuquerque. She reminded herself to thank Vicky for her devoted management of the office.

She returned home and unwound with a glass of wine, then prepared a light dinner and sat down to enjoy her favorite program, *Chopped*, on the Food Network. Among the competitors was a chef from Santa Fe, who won. She made a mental note to check out his restaurant. When the program concluded she turned off the TV and carried her dinner plate to the kitchen sink for a quick rinse.

She glanced out the kitchen window at the cul-de-sac where a police car sat with the engine running. She assumed two cops sat inside and she waved, not certain either of them saw her, then she turned off the kitchen light and walked down the hall to her bedroom.

Officers Derek Vogel and Tony Fuentes sometimes parked in front of her house during a break or to complete paperwork. They and Sally met during an incident shortly after she moved into her newly built home. A runaway drug suspect had tossed a large plastic bag of marijuana out the car window during a chase and the bag landed in her driveway. For a brief upsetting period, Sally was under suspicion as an accomplice. She and the two patrolmen later laughed about it, the scene of Sally being rousted out of bed at sunrise and standing in the driveway in her housecoat and tousled hair, being questioned by two policemen. The three became close friends, and the two cops kept an eye on her and her house to make sure she was okay. On weekends, Sally sometimes invited Tony and Derek in for a fast sandwich or scrambled eggs.

Sitting on the edge of her bed, she rubbed lotion on her hands and face, then reached for the picture of Mike Shannon on the nightstand. The photo was taken three months before the heart attack that took his life, just prior to his retirement from the corporate world and what was to have been their marriage. He was astride his favorite horse, Rusty, with his hands resting on the saddle horn. She kissed the photo and set it back on the nightstand. Then she turned off the light and went to sleep.

∽∽∽∽∽

In Corrales, Midnight was also asleep, perched on the close-to-the-table-top perch. It was the end of his first week in the mew.

The next morning, after John Buscaglia had fed and watered Midnight, he did a quick exam of the large bird. Then he telephoned Kelsey. "Kelsey, great news! Drop whatever you're doing and come on over to help me free Midnight's wing."

Inside the enclosure, they slowly removed the tape from around his body, tape John had changed every day since bringing him home. They set Midnight on the ground of the mew, his body and right wing finally free. For nearly three weeks the wing had been immobilized. He stood still and looked around, then uttered a low *quark* and took a few steps.

Kelsey could sense his mind at work and she jumped when, suddenly, he stood tall and began flapping his wings. He stopped, cocked his head, and answered her squeal with a high-pitched mimicking call.

John observed the scene and smirked. "Kelsey."

She turned. "Yes."

"There's something going on between the two of you." He raised his eyebrows. "Do you think the folks at your trucking company might give you a couple days off?"

"*They*, meaning Sally Tremaine, probably would. Why?"

"I think your friend is going to be ready for release pretty soon.

Three weeks max." He looked east toward the Rio Grande. The terrain from his property sloped down toward the river. "Can we see your place from up here?"

"We sure can." They went outside the mew and she nodded toward the Sandias. "If you drop your line of sight down from Sandia Peak to the river"—she pointed to the peak, several miles to the east—"you'll see a break in the cottonwoods running along the side of the river. In the break is an open field. That's my neighbor, Santiago Gallegos's alfalfa field."

"Okay."

"My house, an adobe with white plaster, is right on the edge of the alfalfa field. We don't have a fence between our properties. Max and I love it. Makes us feel we live on more than our two acres of land."

"What's that small white structure at the corner of the alfalfa field? The corner away from your house."

"That's the chicken house. His pride and joy. He raises Leghorns and Plymouth Rocks. Beautiful chickens. I don't remember the last time I bought grocery store eggs. Mr. Gallegos is a terrific neighbor. Very kind and benevolent." She brushed back a lock of hair. "There's an interesting story about that chicken coop. His dad built a bomb shelter shortly after World War II and placed the chicken coop on top of it."

"No kidding?"

"It was right after the war when folks were experiencing serious war jitters. We had the atomic bomb and so did the Russians. People were afraid we might go to war, and started building bomb shelters to protect themselves and their families. Not many people know about that shelter down there beneath the chicken coop. Just a few of us neighbors. He took me down there one time. The entry door is camouflaged by the coop. Behind the entry door is a small three-bedroom place with a kitchen and a bathroom."

"Fascinating," John said. "Absolutely fascinating." He pondered a moment. "Back to what we were talking about."

"And what was that?" she laughed.

"As close as your home is to mine . . . maybe less than two miles . . ."

"Good estimate."

"If Midnight knew he was welcome at either of our places . . ."

"I see your mind at work."

"I will say no more." He grinned. "If you could help me with Midnight, that would free up more time for me to work with the other birds. And, between us, we could keep up with Midnight and release him as soon as possible."

Kelsey clasped her hands together. "I'll call Sally when I get home."

"In the meantime, could you and Max help me with something else?"

"Of course. Max and I work well together."

"As I've suspected." He chuckled. "Midnight is ready for some roadkill. How familiar are you with roadkill?"

Kelsey let out a whoop. "In my business? Am I familiar with roadkill? Hell yes! See it every day! What kind would you like? And how much?"

"Guess I walked into that one, huh?" He shook his head and grinned. "Any of the non-protected species. Rabbits, coyotes, squirrels, skunks."

"You're on! I'll toss a bucket and shovel in the back of the pickup and go hunting."

Sally readily agreed to Kelsey taking time off to tend to Midnight under John Buscaglia's guidance. "I think what you're doing is wonderful, Kelsey! I'm proud of you."

The following day, Midnight picked up the scent of roadkill from Kelsey's white plastic bucket and began jumping around as she and John approached his enclosure. Kelsey emptied the bucket's contents on the ground and she and John stepped out of the mew. They turned around to watch Midnight leaping from one perch above the table to the other and back again. Then he swept down and attacked the food until it was nearly gone, except for a small portion of the roadkill, which he began to cache beneath one of the rocks in a corner of the mew.

"What a sight," Kelsey said almost in a whisper.

"Amazing, isn't it?" John looked at his watch. "It's late afternoon. I'd like you to go out first thing in the morning and bring back some more roadkill for breakfast. Would you mind?"

"You're serious, aren't you?"

He nodded.

"If my mother could see me now!" She burst out laughing. "I'll be here at sunup with a bucketful."

As she walked back to her pickup in John's driveway, her cell phone rang. She reached for it. "Hello?"

"Hi, Kelsey, this is Rick Delgado. From Taiban. I'm in town. Can I take you to dinner tonight?"

13

Rick leaned back in his chair at the Frontier Bar and Grille in Albuquerque. "So, tell me, Kelsey Brannigan, what have you and Midnight been up to? And, of course, Mr. Max."

Kelsey had noticed a gash across Rick's cheek when they met in the Frontier parking lot. "That's a mean cut on your face, Rick. What happened?"

"I was never good at ducking." He reached forward, placing his hand on hers. "What would you like to drink?" He motioned to the waitress.

"A Coors Light," Kelsey said. It had been a long day and she looked forward to a quiet dinner with Rick. A continuation from where they left off—when he built the chicken wire enclosure for Midnight. She studied the cheek gash and counted at least eight stitches.

The waitress placed two coasters on the weathered-lumber tabletop. "What'll it be, guys?" She was chewing gum and wore large fake eyelashes and a straw cowboy hat.

Rick looked up. "A Coors Light and a Bud."

"What were you ducking from?" Kelsey asked.

"A knife," he said with no facial expression.

"*What!*"

"Big hero." He chuckled. "Tried to break up a fight in a Santa Rosa bar last Saturday."

"My God."

"One of them pulled the knife and I didn't duck fast enough. The crowd jumped him and the fight was over. I apparently left a good bit of blood on the floor of the place." He grinned. "Guess I don't look too cool though, huh?"

"Did someone take you to a hospital?"

"Yeah, they've got a small hospital close by. A cowboy buddy got me over there pronto." Rick glanced down at the cardboard coaster and spun it around. "Fortunately, there was a doctor on duty with experience in sewing people up."

"Are you filing charges?"

"No. The guy doesn't have a pot to put flowers in. I know his dad. And Rick Delgado shouldn't have gotten himself involved trying to break up a couple of drunk young studs bent on destroying each other."

Kelsey looked at him and shook her head as the waitress delivered two bottles of beer and two glasses. "Need anything else?" she asked.

Rick glanced up at her. "No, thanks."

"You poor man," Kelsey said. She reached forward and gently touched his face.

"Thanks."

"Miss Fill and Molly?" she asked. "How are they?"

He took off his hat and set it on one of the side chairs. "They're both fine. Don't know what I'd do without 'em."

"Did you find all your stray cattle?" The waitress placed a basket of corn chips on the table. Kelsey picked up one of the chips.

Rick reached into the basket for a chip and tapped it against Kelsey's. "Found 'em all. That was one god-awful storm."

"Sure as hell was." She picked up another corn chip. "What brings you to Albuquerque?"

"I drove over to take a look at a bull a friend of mine wants to sell. He has a ranch over near Stanley."

"Are you still looking at ranching property near Stanley?"

"Just waiting for a buyer of my Taiban ranch." He toyed with his beer coaster.

She smiled. "I hope it works out."

"Thanks. I do too."

They were silent for a moment, then Kelsey asked, "Is your friend selling the bull an old-time buddy?"

"We went to New Mexico A&M together. It's New Mexico State now." He glanced down at the basket. "How's your pooch?"

She smiled. "That loveable dog. He's my shadow. Always has been."

"Do you truckers get paid by the hour or by the mile?"

"Most truckers are paid by the mile."

"That can cost you when you're stuck in bumper-to bumper traffic."

"Big time." She took a sip of beer. "Big time. I'm fortunate to be driving for a small trucking company where the four of us drivers are salaried. I'm truly blessed."

Rick nodded. "Sounds like you are. How's Midnight coming along?"

She took another sip and set the glass on the table. "Let me bring you up to date on Midnight!" She laughed. "My dear Midnight."

Kelsey told Rick of Midnight's safe passage in the chicken wire cage he built in her 18-wheeler and the physical exam conducted by Kate Harrison. She mentioned Kate's referral to Wildlife Rescue and subsequent progress under the guidance of John Buscaglia. "Its been a fascinating journey, Rick."

"Amazing." His eyes sent congratulations while he ran his fingers across the stitches on his cheek.

"I have the feeling we'll be releasing him back to the wild pretty quickly."

"Do you think he'll return to Taiban?"

"John Buscaglia thinks he'll probably stay in this area, but I don't know."

Rick picked up another corn chip from the basket. "Kelsey, I'm wondering . . ."

"Wondering what?"

"If Midnight were to return to Taiban, is there some way I could identify him if I see him?"

"What a great thought! Let me ask John if maybe we could put a band on one of his legs."

"Maybe John could put a band on one of your legs too."

Kelsey blushed. "What do you mean?"

"In case you ever fly through Taiban again, I can find you."

She laughed. "Now, Rick Delgado, that is a line I've never heard before!"

"Seriously. Do you and your big 18-wheeler ever get over that way?"

"It all depends on scheduling. If I've got anything to or from Texas, I'll likely go that way."

"I'd sure like it if you could stop at my place sometime. I've got a two-bedroom ranch house with plenty of room for you and Max. I know Molly would like to have Max as a guest."

Kelsey emptied her glass and smiled. "I'll think about that, cowboy."

14

"Sally," Vicky called from her desk. "Cliff Atchison on the line."

"Thanks, Vicky." Sally reached for the phone. "Good morning, Cliff."

"Mornin', Sally." Cliff, along with his brother Bobby and sister Kate, were the owners and division heads of Atchison Industries. "I've got a big one for you."

Sally's eyes brightened. "Outstanding!"

"It's on short notice. Like tomorrow. We got caught off-guard with it, but it's a damned good order."

"We'll make it work, Cliff."

"I hope you don't have any other commitments for the next few days."

"All our customers are aware of Doc Morgan Trucking's exclusive with Atchison. You all come first and most of them understand." Sally picked up her pen. "How many loads we looking at?"

"We'll need two of your rigs."

"Not a problem. We'll use Kelsey's rig and the Kenworth. Slim Perkins can handle the other customers with his truck."

"Thanks."

She heard his sigh.

"Can we start loading one of the trucks today?"

She glanced at her watch. "I can drive the Kenworth over right now. Vicky can follow me in one of the pickups and bring me back."

"That'd be great!"

"Then I'll have Kelsey drive her rig over first thing in the morning. Where are we going?"

"Dallas and Fort Worth. Is that OK?"

"We've got you covered, pardner."

∽∽∽∽∽

Kelsey pulled into John Buscaglia's driveway just before sunrise. She hated leaving Max at home, but John was concerned his presence might upset the birds in rehab.

"I understand," Kelsey had replied. "Max has a big fenced yard to run around in and prairie dogs to chase if he gets bored."

She turned off the ignition and stepped out of the truck. The lights were on in John's house. She heard him filling a feed bucket out in the garage and headed in that direction.

"Good morning, John," she said as she opened the side door of the garage.

She saw him bent over a box of strawberries, transferring generous portions into one of two plastic buckets at his feet. In the other bucket were several hard-boiled chicken eggs.

"Good morning." John stood and straightened his back. "Glad you're here. We can feed all the guys together this morning and I'll show you how it's done. Tomorrow, Midnight is all yours."

"Works for me!"

"We'll start with him now." He handed Kelsey the bucket with the hard-boiled eggs. "Let's go."

They approached Midnight's mew. He was by himself. Most of the other enclosures had two to four birds.

Kelsey entered first. Midnight was on the perch just above the table. He jumped down to the top of the table and began preening himself.

When John entered the mew the bird stopped preening and let out a squawk.

John chuckled. "Definitely a male bird."

"How can you tell?" Kelsey said.

"Not difficult. When you entered the mew, our friend began preening himself. When I entered, he squawked at me."

Kelsey laughed.

"Put one of those eggs in that pan on the table. I'll place a few strawberries in this other pan."

She reached out with one of the shelled eggs and placed it in the pan a few feet from Midnight. He muttered a *quark* and walked over to it. Within seconds it was gone.

"Give him another one," John said.

The second egg disappeared as quickly as the first.

~~~~~

Sally was enroute from Santa Fe to Albuquerque in her pickup with Dix in the passenger seat.

Sally retrieved the ringing cell phone from her shirt pocket. "Hello."

"Sally, this is Vicky. I've been trying to get ahold of Kelsey for the past two hours. She might be with her cowboy, Rick. I don't have a clue."

"Did you leave a message on her phone?"

"Three or four messages. Do you remember the name of the guy in Corrales who's helping her with the raven?"

"No, I don't. We're on our way to Albuquerque now. We'll swing by her place on the way."

"Ten-four."

"Vicky, before you hang up . . ."

"Yes."

"If we can't find Kelsey, I might ask Dix to drive our Kenworth and I'll drive Doc's T600. It's in need of a good workout."

"Good idea. Doc would like that."

~~~~~

John Buscaglia and Kelsey finished feeding the birds and cleaning their enclosures by midmorning. "Let's go inside for a cup of coffee," he said, "and I'll share my thoughts with you on Midnight's status."

As they walked down the narrow path toward the house, Kelsey reached in her pocket for her cell phone. "My God, I turned the phone off when I went to bed early last night and forgot to turn it on this morning!"

John chuckled. "That happens when you get older."

She glanced at the phone screen. "Crap. Five messages. One from my mom and four from Vicky at work."

John opened the back door of the house. "While I put a pot of coffee on, you can answer those calls."

"Kelsey, where have you been?" Vicky said. "I've been calling you."

"Sorry, Vicky, I forgot to turn on my phone. Probably should have kept my land line, but it made no sense since I'm on the road so often. What's up?"

"We needed two rigs to make a run to Dallas/Fort Worth. When we couldn't find you, Sally decided to drive Doc's rig with Dix driving their Kenworth."

"I'm so sorry, Vicky."

"Sally and Dix drove by your place early this morning and saw Max in the back yard. They figured maybe you were off with the raven."

"I am. I'm over in Corrales right now. Do you think I should try to contact Sally?"

"No, I'll call her. She'll be glad to know you're okay."

⁓⁓⁓⁓⁓⁓

Sally took the lead in Doc Morgan's metallic-blue 18-wheeler. Dix followed behind her in their larger rig.

Doc had died two years earlier, but Sally wanted to keep the rig with the *Doc Morgan Trucking* lettering on its sides. The parking lot was its home. But insurance and maintenance expenses wouldn't go away. If the right person came along, a driver Doc would like, she'd consider a sale.

She felt Doc's presence in the cab whenever she drove it, her fingers around the steering wheel in the same spots he had held it. She had to scoot the seat forward from his position and raise it a few inches from his setting.

She made a habit of taking the truck out every week or two for a short run on Interstate 40 to make sure the systems and fluids were running as they should. This run to Dallas and Fort Worth would be the first honest-to-goodness long haul for the rig since Doc died. She glanced to her right, expecting to see him in the passenger seat wearing his brown derby with its small red feather.

She turned on the CB and switched to a seldom used channel she and Dix employed from time to time. "You doing okay back there, kiddo?"

"It's kinda lonely driving solo. This big ol' cab is accustomed to having a pilot and a copilot."

"We've been on the road since early morning. Tucumcari is up ahead. Let's take a break."

"Works for me. Have you made contact with Kelsey?"

"Yep. She's OK. She thinks her raven is about ready to return to the wild. I'll bring you up to date when we stop."

"Ten-four."

The moment Dix reached up to place the mic in its slot, the truck lurched to the left and the steering wheel turned violently, forcing her hands free as the truck drove into the earthen median of Interstate 40. It bounced abruptly for several yards, then came to a sudden stop. Fortunately there was no traffic in the left eastbound lane when she shot across it.

Sally had just glanced at her two side rearview mirrors and saw Dix and the Kenworth careening into the median. "Oh, God!" She grabbed the mic. "Dix, I'll exit as quickly as I can and come back to help you." Then she switched to the emergency channel.

"Break, channel nine, this is Hoot N' Holler One. 18-wheeler forced into median, possible mechanical failure, I-40 eastbound near mile-marker three two zero."

"Hoot and Holler," came an immediate reply, "Quay County deputy sheriff. Your location?"

Sally squinted to read the approaching marker on her right. "Hoot N' Holler passing mile marker three-two-two. Will take next exit and return to scene to assist."

"Ten-four."

Dix was uninjured and unshaken and was alarmed at how calm she was as dust rose from all sides. She reached for the mic and switched to channel 9. "Hoot N' Holler One, Hoot N' Holler Two. I'm okay." She turned off the ignition. No smoke or fire was evident—only the billowing dust from the semi's churning of the median's grass and dirt.

In the distance, coming from the direction of Tucumcari, she heard a siren. She opened the door and stepped down. The tractor was tilted to the left and closer to the ground than usual. Cars and other vehicles in both eastbound and westbound lanes were slowing to see what had happened. She glanced down at the left front tire. It had a gaping tear on the side and the truck was resting on the tire rim.

She patted the fender and sighed. "So this is what a blowout looks like. You scared the bejesus out of me, old girl." She laughed and patted the fender again. "But no one got hurt. Wait 'til Sally sees this!"

The deputy sheriff turned off his siren and pulled off the westbound lane of the interstate and into the median. He left his rotating emergency lights on, stopped in front of the Kenworth, then rushed to Dix still standing beside the blown tire. "Are you okay, ma'am?"

"I'm okay. Thanks." She glanced down at the tire. "Think I had a blowout."

He looked at the wrinkled tire rubber resting on the rim. "Yes, ma'am, you sure as hell did. Everything else okay?"

"Yes, thank God."

Dix turned as Sally pulled the T600 to the right side of the westbound lane and ran across the interstate.

"You alright, Dix?" she called as she approached.

"Had a badass blowout, that's all."

"A *badass* blowout! Now you're talking like a trucker, girl!"

"Ladies," the deputy said, "I want to get both of you out of here as quickly as we can. Fortunately, no one's hurt. Are the two of you driving together? In convoy?"

"Yes, we are," Sally said.

"Good." He turned to Dix. "I want you to secure your rig and get in your partner's rig. Then I'm going to escort you to a crossway just a short distance west of here where we'll do a U-turn and head east to Tucumcari to Jack's Truck Repair."

"I'm with you," Sally said.

"We'll ask Jack to send one of his boys out here to tow this rig back to his shop and put on a new tire and send you on your way. Okay?"

"Sounds too easy, Sheriff," Dix said.

The deputy pointed to the traffic slowing in both directions and gawking. "I'm not being easy or trying to be nice. I'm being selfish. I want you both out of here pronto before there's any more accidents. Like right now!"

"Understand," Dix said. She turned to recover personal items from the Kenworth and locked it up.

By midafternoon, Dix and Sally were ready to pull out of Jack's lot with two new front tires on the Kenworth. Close inspection found the right front tire also showing wear.

"Dix," Sally said before they climbed into the trucks, "I've never experienced a blown tire like you just did. You are now a seasoned trucker, girl."

"Correction, Sally. This old gal is now a *badass* seasoned trucker! By the way, after visiting with the tire experts here at Jack's this afternoon, I've got new respect for a rig's tires."

"How's that?"

Dix reached down and patted the driver's side front tire. "The tires are the only part of this machine that touch the road."

"So?"

"They do the *going*, the *stopping*, and the *steering*. Think about it!"

Midnight.

Midnight in the old cottonwood.

Devils Tower.

Midnight and Moses.

15

J OHN BUSCAGLIA AND KELSEY HAD JUST WRAPPED UP THEIR CARE AND FEEDING of the birds.

"Kelsey," John said, as they approached the path back to his house. "Midnight is recovering very quickly. Faster than I'd expected."

"He's an amazing bird, isn't he?"

"I want you to do something." He stopped and turned to the open space between the mews and the dirt road connecting his home to the Rio Grande frontage road and Kelsey's small piece of land on the other side of the river. "Instead of turning right to walk to your pickup in the driveway as you have been doing, I want you to go across that open area and over to the road and head home. By yourself. All of the mews, including Midnight's, face that way. You'll be visible to all the birds as you walk. They'll be watching you."

"Okay. What are we up to, John?"

"Midnight, in particular, will be following your every movement."

"Uh-huh."

"You'll disappear from his view when you reach the Rio Grande and the cottonwoods. That's about a mile and a half. Stop there when you get to the frontage road."

"I'm still not tracking you."

"Hear me out. I'll drive down to pick you up and bring you back to get your truck. Then, Miss Kelsey"—he winked at her—"tomorrow we release Midnight. Right after the morning feeding and you'll walk home once again."

"*Really?*"

"He's ready. In the morning, after his release, I'll want him to see you walking from here down to the river, as you'll do today, then across the bridge and home. He'll be around here someplace—roosting or flying—and he'll decide whether to follow you or not."

She clasped her hands in front of her mouth. "I love it!"

"Of course, I'll drive to your place later to bring you back here for your truck."

"Thank you. I thought you were going to ask me to walk back to get it! This is wild. Totally wild!"

"If he follows you, he'll know he has two safe spots if he ever needs one. This place and yours. Or"—he paused—"he may decide to head east."

"To Taiban."

"Correct. To where you found him. I do want to band him, though." He pulled a bright orange plastic leg band from his pocket and handed it to her. "In case either of us happens to see the old boy sometime. You never know. He might be looking for us."

"A cowboy friend of mine and I were talking about Midnight the other evening when we were having a beer. He wondered if we'd be banding him."

John grinned. "Well, Kelsey, now you can tell that cowpuncher friend of yours we're doing exactly that. You'll notice the band has my name and telephone number on it."

She turned the band over and studied it, then handed it back to him. "Cool!"

"Hold him while I attach it."

Kelsey reached for Midnight on the middle perch and carefully wrapped her hands around him. He uttered a low grunting *bonk*. She held him to her chest while John attached the band to one of his legs.

"Good boy," she said as she returned him to his perch. "Isn't his black sheen beautiful?"

"Sure is. In fact, we all tend to attach a blackness to these beautiful birds, but, if you look closely, you'll see a greenish or purple or blue sheen as well."

She moved closer to Midnight, still on his perch. "You're so right. I'd never realized that." She cocked her head to Midnight. "What a stud you are!"

"Never heard someone call a raven a stud before."

They stepped outside the mew. Kelsey shoved her hands in her back pockets and glanced at the open field. "Well"—she inhaled—"like my mother used to say, 'There's no time like the present.'" She turned and walked toward the open area and called back to him. "Don't forget to drive down to pick me up."

"Don't worry. I'll be there."

When she reached the fence line and changed direction toward the dirt road, she turned to see Midnight on his perch and felt his eyes following her.

Early next morning when she opened John's garage door, she found him emerging from one of the feed bins with a smile on his face. "Today's the day, Kelsey." He placed the lid back on the bin and grinned. "Your boy's release."

"I hope he's regained enough of his strength to hold his own."

"He won't be a hundred percent, but it won't take him long." John put on his Levi jacket. "What I thought we would do is put feed out for Midnight first, then we'll feed the other birds." He buttoned his jacket. The worn copper buttons had their own distinctive patina. "Did you find any roadkill on your way over, by chance?"

"Max and I scooped up a dead rabbit down near the river. I've got the bucket right outside." She reached in her jacket pocket. "I also brought this." She held a hard-boiled egg in her hand.

"Good."

"We'll start with Midnight and come back around to his mew after feeding the others. He should be through eating by then. After we open the front side of his enclosure, you start walking home, and we'll see what happens."

"This is exciting, John." She smiled. "Midnight and I are both in your debt."

He patted her on the shoulder. "I've enjoyed working with you and your raven. It's up to him now to return to the wild and make it on his own."

Feeding completed, they approached Midnight's mew from the front.

"Looks like he ate everything," Kelsey said.

John winked at the bird. "Good boy."

Midnight was on the highest of the perches above the table. He uttered a rolling gurgling sound when John began unlatching one side of the framed screen facing the open field. Kelsey stood on the other side near the screen's hinges. She stepped aside as John swung the side of the mew open.

Midnight took side steps on the perch. He cocked his head and took side steps back again.

"Start walking home as you did yesterday," John said.

She took a few steps down the slope, distancing herself from the mew, then curiosity led her to glance back over her shoulder to see Midnight cocking his head again. Without hesitation, he sprang from his perch and swooped over her head, then lifted skyward, banking into a giant circle high above. Her face flushed and goose bumps covered her entire body.

She continued walking, at a faster pace than she did the day before.

When she reached the end of John's property and the path turned toward the dirt road, she looked up to the sound of *quorks*. Midnight was still flying in a wide circle high above. She noticed two other ravens flying nearby, observing this newcomer to the neighborhood.

"Searching the sky," Kelsey said when John picked her up to return for her pickup. "I saw six or eight ravens diving and chasing one another. Two of them left the group to check out Midnight. When they apparently found he wasn't part of their family they rejoined their group and went on."

"I saw that, too," he said. "He tried to keep up with them, but he didn't have the strength or the stamina. It'll take him a little time to regain his oomph. He flew on alone. Toward Sandia Mountain. Then I lost him."

16

OFFICERS TONY FUENTES AND DEREK VOGEL DROVE INTO SALLY TREMAINE'S cul-de-sac to spend a few minutes completing paperwork on two traffic stops. It was long after dark.

Tony was driving. "There's a car parked in front of Sally's house. She and Dix are in Dallas, aren't they?"

"That's what she told us. Pull up behind him," Derek said. "Damned tinted windows!" he growled. "Can't tell if it's a male driver or a woman."

Tony eased around the cul-de-sac and stopped behind the black Range Rover. "California plates."

He reached for his lapel mic. "I'll ask Dispatch to run a plate check."

As he completed his conversation with Dispatch, the driver of the Range Rover started the engine and pulled away.

"I'll tail him at a distance," Tony said.

Within seconds they listened to the report from Dispatch: "Vehicle owned by Jake Brattan. Shows two addresses. One in Los Angeles. The other in Pahrump, Nevada. Convicted felon. Served time at Cañon City."

Derek keyed his mic. "Thanks, Dispatch." He was silent a moment. "I don't like the sound of that. Let's get ahold of Sally after she returns home. See if she knows anything about this guy."

∞∞∞∞∞

Sally and Dix spent the night in Big Spring, Texas, and got up the next morning to continue to Fort Worth.

Over breakfast, Sally asked Dix, "Do you want to take the lead today, and I'll be the caboose?"

"No thank you. I'm happy as I can be bringing up the rear. All I've got to think about is keeping your tractor and trailer in sight and following it wherever it goes. You're the one making the decisions about how fast we're goin' and which way to turn."

Sally patted her arm. "Thanks for your confidence." She took a sip of coffee. "I was thinking about the two of us while I was taking a shower this morning. We've come a long way, haven't we?"

"Two gals in their fifties deciding to become truckers. Unbelievable." She looked down and played with the corner of her place mat. "Most women our age would have preferred something more sensible. Like working at a desk. Or knitting."

"Speaking of women truckers, I think the Great American Truck Show is being held in Dallas this week."

"GATS? No kidding?"

"At the Kay Bailey Hutchison Convention Center."

"Let's swing by and catch the excitement before we head back home. Women in Trucking has a booth every year. And you and I *are* members."

"That would be great! Ellen Voie should be there."

"Ellen is my hero," Dix said. "Started Women in Trucking all by herself, with Char Pingel riding shotgun."

"Two amazing women."

"I wonder what the parking situation is at the convention center."

"Don't forget we've got two rigs."

"Lordy," Dix said, "if it's a trucking show there's got to be parking for trucks!"

"We can leave one rig in the motel parking lot. Maybe the Kenworth. Doc's truck is easier to park. Let's drive it to the show."

Dix raised her hand for a high five.

They found a spot for Doc's rig in a football field-sized parking lot behind the center and walked around the building to the front entrance.

Dix pressed her hands against her cheeks when they were inside. "My God!" She took a deep breath. "This is the biggest building I've ever seen in my life!"

Sally stood beside her, flipping through the pages of the program. "You won't believe the things they've got going on. Alex Debogorski, *the* Ice Road Trucker, is here!"

"That man is an honest-to-God *character*. Have you ever seen him on television?"

"A couple years ago. Those ice road truckers are something else, driving their heavy rigs on that Arctic ice."

"Both men and women drivers."

"A few have ended up at the bottom of riverbeds and lakebeds." Sally turned another page of the program. "Meredith Ochs and SiriusXM Radio are here, too!"

"We've listened to Meredith lots of times. We've *got* to visit her booth!"

Sally pointed straight ahead. "There's the Women in Trucking table. I see Ellen. Let's start there."

"Right on!"

Three hours later they sat at one of the cafeteria tables near the edge of the lobby. Sally set her paper napkin down beside the white plastic plate as her cell phone rang.

"Hello," she said. "Derek Vogel. What a surprise to hear from you."

Dix put her cup of coffee down and fixed her eyes on Sally.

"We're in Dallas," Sally said. "At the truck show. We'll be heading home as soon as we drive to the motel parking lot and pick up the other rig. I know you aren't calling me to discuss the weather. What's up?" She pulled a small notepad from her shirt pocket. Then her pen. She pressed the cell phone against her ear. "What!" She frowned. "Jake Brattan? Yeah, I know who he is." She glanced up at Dix. "In front of my house? That bastard!" She rubbed her forehead. "You bet, Derek. I'll check in with you as soon as we get home."

Sally placed the cell phone on the table and raised her eyes to meet Dix's. "Derek and Tony found a car parked in front of my house last night and ran a check. It was Jake Brattan."

Dix frowned.

"They were going to wait 'til we got back to talk about it. Then they began to worry and decided to call me now."

"What are you going to do?"

"I don't know. The son of a bitch has definitely stepped over the line." She glanced across the lobby at people milling around and visiting.

"Maybe have him tailed. Substantiate stalking or harassment." She turned back to Dix. "Build on the case that got him slapped in prison."

"Cutting our brake lines, then the bastard sabotaged our engine up in Wyoming."

17

THE MORNING KELSEY CLIMBED THE SOUTH SIDE OF RATON PASS ON Interstate 25, traffic was light, and it was also fast. The trailer carried a full load of equipment from Atchison Industries for delivery to the University of Colorado in Boulder. She remained in the right lane while cars, pickups, and a few 18-wheelers passed on her left. Most of the 4-wheelers ignored the 75 MPH speed limit. Max was curled up on the passenger seat.

Descending on the north side just inside the Colorado line, she gained speed while moderate crosswinds jostled the rig. The full load minimized any concern about the rig's stability.

On the right shoulder, not far from a creek bed below, she saw a dead deer, probably hit during the night. She recalled a recent newspaper article naming Raton Pass as one of the most crash-prone roads in the region for wildlife. Glancing at the carcass in the right rearview mirror, she murmured, "I feel sorry for you, Mr. Deer, and I wish I could somehow contact Midnight and his raven friends. You'd provide them with a pretty stout breakfast."

During the climb up the gradual rise outside Trinidad, she slowed the truck's speed. She glanced ahead to the left. Coming toward her in one of the southbound lanes, a black-colored rig was starting to fishtail. Forty tons at seventy miles an hour. "My God, driver, slow down!" she called out.

Max sat up in his seat and looked around with his ears back.

Kelsey glanced over at the older driver fighting to bring the giant machine under control. The rig bounced off the concrete median and careened to the right. In her left-side mirror, she watched the rear end of the truck whip to the side as the tractor trailer tumbled off the interstate. She saw no other collisions; however, the mirror became a solid sea of red brake lights.

She reached above for her mic, switched to emergency channel 9, and keyed the mic. "Emergency! This is Bronco Brannigan, I-25 near Trinidad. 18-wheeler rollover between exits two-three and two-seven southbound."

"Brannigan," came a response, "this is Colorado State Patrol. Your location?"

"Brannigan is northbound I-25. Just witnessed a rig hit the median and ricochet off the side of the interstate. Southbound traffic is backing up at the scene. There's no way for me to get over there to assist." She watched two southbound 18-wheelers slowing down.

"This is Texas Pete southbound," came the radio. "Approaching the rollover."

"Roger, Texas Pete. Colorado Patrol. I'm approaching the scene behind you. Thanks, Brannigan."

Kelsey keyed her mic. "Ten-four. Brannigan out."

By the time she reached Colorado Springs, Kelsey learned on the CB that the fifty-eight-year-old driver from Arizona had been transported to a Pueblo, Colorado hospital and died en route. When she heard the news, she reached up and pulled the air horn lanyard to help him on his journey to the other side.

After the University of Colorado delivery, she and Max spent the night in Boulder at a well-known motel that accommodated truckers with their tractors and long trailers.

Off and on during the night Kelsey thought about Midnight—how was he? Where was he?—and decided to detour through Taiban on the return home to Corrales, even though the detour would add an hour to the return journey. She might find him. She might not. The odds were against her, but she felt compelled to try.

Boulder was beginning to awaken when she and Max climbed into the cab. It wouldn't be long before commuter traffic to Denver would be at full strength.

Approaching Taiban from the west, she saw the railroad tracks to her right and Fort Sumner a few miles behind her. In the distance, the weather-worn Presbyterian church came into view. Behind it, further away, she saw the faint outline of Rick Delgado's ranch house and barn.

The few outlying buildings of what was once a thriving Taiban all appeared to be empty. Atop one building, Kelsey noticed the sign for a volunteer fire department. But not a living creature was in sight. She drove past the empty buildings and left the highway, turning onto the familiar dirt road, which ran a short distance to the church and abruptly ended behind it. She drove slowly to the rear and turned the rig around to face the highway. The sun was directly overhead.

By this time, Max was standing in the passenger seat and eyeing Kelsey with a *Please open the window on my side* look on his furry face. Kelsey grinned and lowered the window, then slowed the truck to a stop. She cut the engine and scanned the area for signs of ravens or any other birds. There were none. She opened the driver's side door and she and Max exited the truck to search and explore.

Max reconnoitered the area and trotted over to the church to sniff around the steps and the dark area beneath the dilapidated floor. Kelsey noticed the long narrow board she had used to scoot food and water to Midnight. It rested beside the steps, caked in dust and dirt. The imprint of the tarp she had lain on was still visible.

She looked upward, searching the sky and rooftops for any sign of ravens.

"*Miiidnight,*" she called. "*Miiidnight.*"

She followed two ravens circling lazily above in the random wind drafts and currents. Neither bird paid any attention to her calls.

She continued searching and calling for nearly an hour. There was no sign of Midnight.

"Max, I told Vicky we'd be back home before nightfall. Let's grab a bite, then head out."

Max looked up at her and wagged his tail.

The only sound they heard was vehicle traffic on Highway 84. Until, from behind, she and Max turned around to the sound of a horse's neigh. Riding tall in Miss Fill's saddle was Rick Delgado, waving. Molly ran alongside.

Max ran out to meet Molly while Kelsey stood waiting with her hands in her back pockets. A crosswind dropped a lock of hair across her forehead.

"What brings you way out to Taiban?" Rick asked as he eased out of the saddle.

"Max and I are returning from a delivery in Colorado. Curiosity got the best of me. Thought I'd drop by to see if Midnight had come back."

He took off his hat and wiped his brow with a handkerchief. "Any luck?"

She shook her head. "Nope. But he's been on my mind. I hope he's okay."

"Had lunch yet?"

"No, I'm going to make myself a sandwich up in the crew cab kitchen." She glanced up at the cab. "Then Max and I are pulling out. Can I make something for you?"

Rick nodded toward his ranch house. "Why don't you drive your truck over to my place and we can put something together in a real kitchen?"

Kelsey glanced at his house and paused. "How would I get this big 18-wheeler from here to there?"

"The gate to my back-road entrance is right over there." He pointed to the corral. "Only a few folks know about it. Just follow Miss Fill and me."

"I can't stay long."

18

Inside, on his king-sized bed, Kelsey rested her head against Rick's shoulder, enjoying the moment and the comfort of his arm wrapped around her. She visualized Miss Fill swatting flies with her long graceful tail while she grazed in the open field surrounding Rick's home and she pictured Max and Molly dozing in the shade of the front porch. The mournful wail of a westbound freight train broke the early afternoon silence.

She opened her eyes to the narrow ray of sunlight beaming through the open edge of the bedroom curtains. "I need to be going, Rick."

"I don't want you to leave, Kelsey," he whispered.

She sighed and rolled over. "We both have work to do, cowboy." She inched across the bed and sat on its edge for a few seconds, then reached for her clothes scattered on the floor and a side chair.

Rick rolled to face her and propped his head on an elbow. "Are you ever going to settle down?"

Kelsey hooked her bra behind her back, then reached for her pearl-button shirt. "What do you mean?"

"Like maybe get married. Have a house full of kids. And a husband." He scooted to the side of the bed and dropped his bare legs over the side, touching hers. "Maybe a husband named Rick Delgado."

She glanced at him and grinned. "Is that a proposal?" She poked the end of his nose with her finger, then reached for her jeans.

"Sort of."

"You remind me of someone else I once knew." She started buttoning her jeans. "We were in the same transportation company in Iraq. I suspect he's still in the Army."

"How do I remind you of him?"

"He wanted me to marry him so we could have a houseful of kids."

"You're a free spirit, aren't you, Kelsey? Princess Diana of the plains."

"And you, my friend, are a poet." She ran her fingers through her hair. "I wasn't ready at the time. I'm still not ready."

"How come? You want to become a crotchety old maid surrounded by her cats?"

"What you men don't understand is that it's the woman who endures the discomfort of pregnancy and the pain of childbirth. It's the woman who raises and nurtures the children. And I fully understand that. I get it." She sighed. "I get those maternal yearnings from time to time, as any woman does. They're part of life. One day they'll probably be part of *my* life. But just not yet."

"And the man? What's he doing all this time?" He wrapped his arms across his bare chest. "Damn, I'm getting cold." He rose from the side of the bed and walked around to the other side, picking up his clothes along the way.

"The man just waits for the next roll in the hay and making more babies." She stood and buckled her belt with its oval-shaped rodeo buckle.

"We don't have to have kids right away." He pulled his Levis on. "Or ever, as far as that goes."

"That's quite a concession, Rick." She pulled on her boots.

"I mean it. No kids unless and until we both want them."

"This is sounding better." She walked over and put her arms around him and kissed him on the lips. "Let's keep the subject open."

He held her tightly. "You're on."

"Max and I need to get back on the road," she said softly. "We have work to do." She walked to the bedroom door, turned with a wink, and left.

"I hope you find Midnight!" he called after her.

Kelsey and Max climbed aboard the rig and she strapped in while Max took his spot in the passenger seat. She started the engine and released the brake, then glanced over her shoulder at the second-floor window where Rick stood watching. She reached up to the air horn lanyard and gave him two quick bursts and pulled away.

19

K ELSEY POURED HERSELF A CUP OF COFFEE AND JOINED DIX, SLIM, AND VICKY at the conference room table in Sally's office.

"It's been a long time since we've all been in town at the same time." Sally glanced around at everyone. "I've got nothing earthshaking to share with you this morning. I just want to seize the opportunity to bring everyone up to date on Doc Morgan Trucking and how we're doing as a company. This will take an hour or so. Afterwards we'll go out for lunch together."

Kelsey's cell phone began vibrating in her belt holster. She pulled it out and checked the screen. John Buscaglia. She slipped the phone back into the holster.

"Something you need to tend to?" Sally looked over the top of her glasses.

"It can wait." *Why is John calling? News of Midnight?* It has to be. Kelsey retrieved the phone again and turned it off. She'd forgotten Sally wanted cell phones turned off during meetings. All phones except Vicky's. Vicky, the primary point of contact for the company for every*one* and every*thing*.

"Our exclusive contract with Atchison Industries continues to be Doc Morgan Trucking's bread and butter," Sally reported. "Thank you all for your dedication to the Atchison relationship and for responding to Vicky's calls—sometimes on short notice."

Vicky was seated beside Sally. "You're all a joy to work with." Kelsey noticed Vicky retrieve a small recorder from a shirt pocket. "If you don't mind, I'm not going to depend on myself to take notes today. I've got a sinus headache that kept me up half the night." She placed the recorder in front of her and turned it on. "Going to let the recorder do the work."

"If Doc was here, he'd pull some medicine out of his desk drawer for you," Dix said.

"I know," Vicky answered.

Kelsey noticed Slim, seated across the table, wink at Vicky in understanding.

"I wanted all of you to know," Sally continued, "that I've decided to list Doc's T600 for sale. It's a difficult decision, but we're not driving the rig often enough to keep it in top running condition. And, as we all know, maintenance and insurance costs have a way of adding up. If any of you know of a driver who might be interested, please let me know. The buyer will have to be the right one to be given the keys to Doc's rig." She glanced outside to where it was parked in the first slot in front of the building. "I know you understand."

Everyone nodded.

〰〰〰〰

Dix, sitting on the other side of Sally from Vicky, listened to Sally's succinct presentation and felt pride in what she and Sally had accomplished since Slim taught them to drive a rig and assisted them in the purchase of their own rig. She knew that Sally's decision to sell Doc's truck was a painful one. One of the things that kept the memory of Doc Morgan alive was the presence of his rig out front. Dix also knew that Doc, a business person like Sally, would agree with her decision.

Dix's greatest concern, however, was Sally's safety from the threatening menace of Jake Brattan.

〰〰〰〰

"My final item," Sally said, glancing down at her notes, "is a word of thanks to each of you." She went around the table: "Vicky, for your superb management of the office and your four difficult drivers." She smiled. "Kelsey, for your service to our country as an Army trucker in Iraq and your return to the civilian sector as a crack driver. I'd put your driving skills against anyone on the road, man or woman. Slim, for teaching Dix and me to become truckers and for responding to calls any time of the day or night. Dix, for your steadfast loyalty, your being the best driving partner on the planet, and for your treasured friendship." She closed the tan leather folder in front of her. "Let's go to lunch."

"Before we adjourn, Sally," Kelsey said, "this meeting has been very informative and, as you said at the beginning, it provided a chance for all of us to get together—which, with our busy scheduling, is a rarity. But the tone of your remarks has been, to me at least, almost funereal. Like a closing ceremony of some sort. Is there something you're not telling us?"

Sally took off her reading glasses and smiled at Kelsey. "There's a personal issue I'm dealing with, Kelsey, and it'll be resolved." She paused. "It has nothing to do with my health or any of you or Doc Morgan Trucking. I promise." She glanced around at everyone. "And I apologize if I may have come across this morning as somewhat distracted. As all our mothers used to tell us, *This, too, shall pass.*" She slipped the glasses in their case. "I'm hungry. Let's go eat."

As Sally stood and walked toward her office door, Kelsey noticed Dix glancing down at the nose of an ankle holster protruding from beneath Sally's jeans.

20

SLIM PLACED HIS HAND ON KELSEY'S SHOULDER AS THEY LEFT THE MEETING. "Why don't you leave your pickup here? We can go to lunch in mine and I'll bring you back."

"Okay, that's kind of you. I have to make a phone call though. Would you mind if I take care of it while you're driving?"

"Not at all."

"John Buscaglia of Wildlife Rescue called me during the meeting. I'll check his message and call him back. It may be about Midnight."

"Your raven?"

"Yeah."

"I love it." He opened the passenger side door of the truck. "Hop in."

Kelsey tapped the message bar and pressed the phone against her ear. *"Kelsey, this is John Buscaglia. Thought you'd want to know I saw Midnight early this morning. Call me back."*

"Wow!" She turned to Slim as he turned the ignition. "John saw Midnight this morning!"

"That's great news!"

She pulled John's number up on the screen and hit "send."

He picked up immediately. "Like I said in my message, Kelsey, our friend Midnight dropped by early this morning while I was feeding the birds. I couldn't believe it. He was perched up on a high branch of the dead cottonwood."

"Oh my God, John! How did he look?"

"He looked fine. And healthy. I grabbed my binoculars and I could see the orange leg band we put on. I think he's fully recovered from his injured wing."

"What was he doing when you saw him?"

"Just looking around. Observing, you know. Checking things out."

"Did he see you?"

"He sure did. In fact, when I went from the first mew to the second one, I glanced up at him, thinking he might fly away. But he just watched me. Turned his head from side to side. He may have been searching for both of us. His feathers were ruffled by the wind."

"This is so exciting!"

"While I was in the second mew feeding two young crows, he looked around some more, then he flew off."

"John, thank you so much for letting me know."

He laughed. "I thought you'd be interested."

"May I come over tomorrow morning for the early feeding? He might come back."

"You bet. Come on over."

"I'll be there." She returned the phone to its holster, then took a deep breath and let it out.

Slim had just entered Interstate 40 heading toward downtown Albuquerque and the El Pinto Restaurant on 4th Street. "Sounded like good news."

"It *was* good news. Midnight is safe. And he's returned to the area." She held her hands together on her lap. "Now that I think about it, maybe he never left. I'm joining John for the early morning feed tomorrow."

"I'm happy for you, Kelsey." He turned. "There's something I want to ask you before we get to lunch. I need your input."

She furrowed her brow. "About what?"

Slim studied the highway. "You're our newest driver. The youngest of Sally, Dix, you, and me. You are also one of the best big rig drivers I've ever known. A true gear-jammer."

"Thank you, Slim."

"Also *battle*-seasoned, I might add. There aren't many civilian truckers who can say that."

"Slim Perkins, you sly devil." She broke out in a laugh. "What are you leading up to?"

He glanced at her. "I'm going to be leaving. Moving back to Austin. At month's end."

Her eyes widened. "*You're what?*"

He checked the rearview mirror, then looked ahead. "I'm thinking of telling Sally and the others at lunch. That's where I need your advice."

"Okay." She glanced at him. "I appreciate your trust and confidence."

"My dad has been an independent trucker for as long as I can remember. He's owned two rigs all this time—one for large jobs and a smaller one for easy, short-distance jobs. Sometimes he takes on a temporary driver, but usually he's been on his own."

"That's how you were introduced to the business?"

"That's right." He paused. "Dad has always been a big strong, husky guy, but recently his health has begun to suffer. A combination of too many cigarettes, a deep attachment to strong drink, and age. He just turned sixty-three this past month. I went home for his birthday. He and Mom really leaned on me to come back home and take over the business."

"That puts a lot of pressure on you, doesn't it?"

"In a sense, yes. I feel very close to you and Sally and Dix and Vicky. I truly believe in Doc Morgan Trucking and was devoted to Doc."

"I'm sorry I didn't get a chance to know him."

"And I love my mom and dad." He hit the turn signal and passed a slow-moving school bus. "Bottom line: Old Slim had to make a decision."

"To return home."

"Yep!"

"Will your sweet wife, Alexis, be going with you?"

"Absolutely!"

Kelsey reached over and patted him on the shoulder.

He glanced at her. "I trust your instinct and your judgment. Is today's lunch the appropriate time and place to tell everyone?"

"Slim, I think it's the perfect time and place."

"How will Sally take it?"

"Sally's a veteran of the business world. She's made moves like yours during her career. Changing saddles, if you will." She smiled. "She's a professional who'll understand and give you her sincere best wishes. I know she will."

〜〜〜〜〜

Following lunch, Sally and Vicky returned to the office to tie up a few loose ends and catch up on paperwork. Dix tagged along with them since she and Sally would be driving back to Santa Fe together.

"That was a surprise announcement from Slim," Sally said as she drove down 4th Street to Interstate 40. "I'll miss him. He's a strong and dependable driver."

"And he taught you and me to drive," Dix said. "Bless his heart, you and I are truckers thanks to that young man."

"Will you try to find another driver to replace him?" Vicky asked.

"We have to. The Atchison relationship is too important for us to do otherwise."

"Any ideas of other drivers?" Dix asked from the back seat.

"I'll put some feelers out. Both of you tell me if you know of anyone we should visit with."

"Man or woman?" Vicky asked.

"Either, but I prefer a man to balance things out, and particularly for our occasional tough runs, like Slim took from time to time."

Several minutes later, they arrived at the office parking lot. Slim waved to them as he pulled out in his pickup and left. Kelsey was opening the door to her truck and was about to get in when Sally hit her horn and motioned to her to wait.

Sally pulled into her parking slot and cut the engine and Kelsey walked over. Sally got out and took her arm. "Your driver networks are broader than mine or Dix's, Kelsey. If you could give some thought to drivers who might be interested in joining us, I'd like to contact them."

"That's been on my mind the past several minutes, Sally. Matter of fact, there are a couple. One in particular, if he'd consider a move."

Vicky and Dix were heading toward the office, but turned around and came back to listen to the conversation.

Sally's eyes lit up. "Can you give me a hint?"

"His name is Bill Gentry. When he's not trucking, he rides the rodeo circuit."

"Like Bronco Brannigan does from time to time?"

"Yup. Buffalo Bill Gentry rides broncs. Bareback." Kelsey folded her arms across her chest. "Tall, white hair, neatly trimmed moustache and beard. Nicest guy in the world unless you piss him off. He kicked another driver's ass across a parking lot a while back when the asshole was threatening Max and me."

Sally turned to Dix. "Remember that hellacious dust storm between Phoenix and Gila Bend several years ago? We met a big man named Buffalo. Definitely a take-charge kind of guy. I'll never forget him."

"He drove for Schneider. The Big Orange."

"His handle was *Buffalo*. We've chatted a few times on the CB since then."

Kelsey interrupted. "Bill Gentry's handle is also *Buffalo*."

"Well, heavenly days!" Dix said.

Sally began laughing. "Kelsey, you are a piece of work! Do you have any plans right now?"

Kelsey grinned. "I don't have any plans until tomorrow morning at sunrise."

"Come inside. Let's see if we can contact Bill Gentry."

Dix and Vicky followed. Dix put her arm around Vicky's waist. "This is fun."

∽∽∽∽∽

That night before she went to bed, Sally glanced out the kitchen window after turning off the ceiling lights. She saw a black Range Rover with tinted windows parked in the cul-de-sac. Its lights were off.

21

KELSEY JUMPED AND MAX WENT FLYING OFF THE BED WHEN THE RAUCOUS alarm clock cut loose at 4:30 A.M.

By 5:30, Max was working on a steak bone Kelsey had been keeping in the fridge. A bone she saved from a recent steak dinner with Rick Delgado. She stood for a few moments to watch him stretched out on the back porch of the house holding the bone with his front paws and chewing away before she closed up the house and drove over the Rio Grande bridge to John Buscaglia's for the early morning feed. In the rearview mirror, the Sandia Mountains outlined the first signs of morning light.

She parked on the side of the dirt road in front of John's house and picked up her binoculars from the passenger seat. She lowered the leather neck strap over her head and closed the truck door, then walked down the driveway. She could see the light on in the garage and heard John rustling among the feed bins. She opened the side door of the garage and whistled to him as he worked at the rear of the garage.

He looked up. "Kelsey! Just in time! I'm almost ready to take breakfast out to our feathered friends. You can help me."

She proceeded to the work table where he had arranged breakfast for his raptor and corvid guests.

"I have three new birds," he said. "They've come in since you were here last. I've also released a couple that were fully recovered. A red-tailed hawk and a raven."

"Congratulations!" She glanced at John's already stained and dusty work clothes. "I sure hope we see Midnight this morning."

"I do, too." He pointed to the far end of the table. "Grab that box of feed tins and I'll take this one." He picked up the larger cardboard box and they headed downhill to the mews. Almost in unison, they glanced at the skeletal cottonwood tree at the rear of his property. No sign yet of Midnight.

They fed two young ravens rehabilitating in the first mew and proceeded to the adjacent mew holding an injured horned owl. Kelsey was watching John feed the owl when he squinted at the upper portion of the cottonwood. "There he is."

Kelsey turned. Perched on a high branch was Midnight, his tail resting against a lower branch! His back was facing them and he was looking away from the tree in the direction of her house and the Rio Grande. She lifted the binoculars and turned the adjustment knob. "My God, John, that's him," she whispered. "I can see the orange leg band." She lifted the strap over her head and handed the binoculars to him.

He held the binoculars against his eyes and made a minor adjustment with the knob. "You're right, young lady! That's Midnight." He continued to study the bird. "Ease out the door, Kelsey, and stand ten or twelve feet from the mew. Just stand there facing him and let's see what he does." He lowered the glasses and winked at her.

"Your wink reminds me of my dad." She lifted the latch and opened the weathered wooden door and eased out. She took four steps into the open desert terrain, then turned toward Midnight. He rotated around on the branch and faced her, then cocked his head and waited, nonchalantly scratching himself beneath a wing with his beak. He stopped scratching and stared at her once again.

Kelsey lifted her hand and rubbed her cheek. She lowered it to her side while Midnight watched her from the cottonwood and took a few side steps on the branch and stopped. He turned to her and let out an undulating *quork*.

"Answer him back," John said from inside the mew.

Kelsey tried, as best she could, to mimic the *quork*.

Midnight turned his head from side to side and made a short series of *caulks*.

Kelsey responded.

Midnight puffed himself out and made another *quork*. Then he stretched one leg and a wing on one side and did the same on the other side. He preened for a few moments and took off—flying east toward the Rio Grande.

John stepped out of the mew. "I've never seen anything like that in my life."

"I am one gigantic goose bump, John. One gigantic goose bump."

"Let's both keep our eyes and ears open. He may be defining his territory with both of us a part of it. I'll let you know if he returns."

"Utterly amazing."

"Can you come back for tomorrow's early feeding?"

"I can't, John. I'm trucking a shipment to Manhattan."

"New York City?" His dark Italian eyes widened.

"No. Manhattan, Kansas. Kansas State University."

He chuckled. "I sometimes forget you have another job. I've gotten used to your help as an associate in all of this."

"I enjoy working with you, John, and I'm learning a lot. But, yes, I do need to earn a paycheck."

"Please get in touch with me as soon as you get back. I'll try, in the meantime, to keep the dialogue going with our friend up in the tree."

22

OFF-LOADING AND INSTALLING THE KANSAS STATE LAB EQUIPMENT PROVED to be more challenging and time-consuming than Kelsey had anticipated. When the task was completed, she contacted a Kansas broker friend who arranged to have an Albuquerque load awaiting her at a warehouse on the other side of Manhattan.

She drove across town, loaded the shipment, and headed home with the trailer packed with merchandise for delivery to a department store on the west side of Albuquerque. This helped the trucking company bottom line as well as her paycheck.

Though she was tired, Kelsey decided to begin the return journey as soon as the trailer doors were closed and locked.

∽∽∽∽∽

In Corrales, John Buscaglia stood at his kitchen sink rinsing the dinner dishes when the telephone rang. He picked up the cordless phone. "Hello." He pressed it against his ear. "Kelsey?"

"John, I couldn't wait any longer. Had to call you. It's been two days since I left. How's Midnight? Have you seen him again?"

"Whoa, young lady! Slow down. Are you driving?"

"No, we're gassing up in Manhattan. Heading back home. Should be back tomorrow. Any news on Midnight?"

"Who are *we*? Who's with you?"

"Aren't you the nosy one! *We* are Max and me. Now, dammit, tell me about Midnight!"

"There was no sign of Midnight yesterday or the day before. But he was back this morning." John was silent for a moment. "I hear a lot of truck noise wherever you are. Are you at one of those big truck stops?"

"Yeah, big truck stop." There was impatience in Kelsey's voice. "Did you and Midnight talk back and forth? Like he and I did?"

"As a matter of fact, we did. It was interesting, Kelsey. Kind of fun.

We chatted back and forth a little longer than you did. Mimicking each other. Then he flew off. In the same direction he did before. East toward the Rio Grande. And your place."

"Outstanding! I'll call you when I get back."

"Okay. Oh, Kelsey?"

"Yes."

"I almost forgot to tell you. There was another raven with him."

"My God! Really?"

"Possibly a female partner." He laughed. "Your boy Midnight doesn't waste any time."

"I can't believe it!"

∽∽∽∽∽

There was a full moon and a cloudless sky, making the nighttime driving easier. Max curled up on the passenger seat as they headed west on Interstate 70. After driving several miles, Kelsey was thirsty and hungry. No doubt Max could be coaxed to eat something as well. She pulled off the interstate at Junction City, grabbed a takeout burger at a truck stop, opened a can of dog food for Max, and got back on the highway.

They passed by the Eisenhower Presidential Library in Abilene and cruised through other Kansas towns and cities as Kelsey flipped back and forth between nighttime trucker radio channels and occasional chats with other truckers on the CB.

As they approached mile marker 265 outside Soloman, Max stood up on the seat and stretched, a sign he might need to jump out of the truck for a few minutes. Kelsey reached over and scratched his head, then downshifted and slowed as they approached an easily accessible moon-lit rest stop. There were no other rigs or 4-wheelers, meaning a quick in and out. She pulled up to the curb and turned off the ignition and reached for the can of Mace on the dashboard. She slipped it into a shirt pocket and opened the door, then lifted Max out of the cab. She watched him dash for the closest bush then follow her to the ladies' restroom where he busied himself exploring the surroundings.

She heard another rig pull up and stop outside. Its engine kept running for a few seconds before being turned off. She buttoned up and opened the stall door, then heard the sound of footsteps approaching from the outside. Suddenly they stopped. Max began to growl.

"What is it, boy?" She heard a toilet flush in the men's room on the other side of the wall. Max uttered a low growl as she walked to the sink to wash her hands.

Then the lights went out. All of them! She pictured some son of a bitch cutting a cable or pulling the master switch. The only light came from moonlight hitting the skylight in the center of the ceiling. Max began growling louder as footsteps approached once again. Kelsey pulled the can of Mace out of her pocket and eased toward the restroom exit. She was within a few feet of the outside when a heavyset man in a tank top stepped in front of her.

"We meet again, bitch," he snarled and reached for her.

In an instant Kelsey had the can of Mace in his face, spraying it directly into his eyes. He tried to push her away with his left hand and attempted to shield his eyes from the poisonous spray with his right. And then she saw it—the black swastika!

"You fucking bastard!" Kelsey screamed while Max dug his teeth into the man's leg.

He screamed and stumbled away and Kelsey and Max dashed to the truck, climbed in, and locked it. She started the engine and backed out, then turned and exited the parking area, glancing toward the restroom building where the swastika slob was trying to find the entry to one of the restrooms.

Kelsey and Max both trembled off and on for the remainder of the night and morning before arriving home totally drained. She parked the trailer at the rear-of-the-building loading ramp of the department store on Albuquerque's west side—for unloading by store workers—then she and Max continued in the tractor to the Doc Morgan parking lot and got in her pickup.

Following the exhausting all-night drive, she napped off and on during the day and went to bed early. Around midnight she woke up to flashing lights of police cars and fire trucks in front of her property and Mr. Gallegos's next door.

23

KELSEY DRESSED AND WENT OUTSIDE. NOSE FIRST IN THE DRY DITCH running in front of her house was an old-model Buick with its doors flung open. It rested against the culvert running beneath the driveway of her next-door neighbor, Mr. Gallegos. Someone attempting to turn in to his driveway obviously didn't make it. Two policemen were examining the car.

A New Mexico State policeman motioned to her and walked over. His name tag read *Sullivan*. "Is this your home, ma'am?"

"It sure is."

"Your name?"

"Kelsey Brannigan. What's going on?"

"There was a breakout at the Metropolitan Detention Center this evening. Two escapees. We have reason to believe they may be holed up on your property or the property next door."

Kelsey's eyes widened. "Oh, my God! I don't understand! Why would two escapees be on my property or Mr. Gallegos's?"

He motioned to another patrolman nearby. The patrolman walked over and stood beside him. "This lady, Kelsey Brannigan, is the home-owner of this property." He pointed to Kelsey's house. "Advise the units."

The patrolmen took a few steps away and radioed the information to police and fire units standing by.

Sullivan turned back. "That abandoned car," he nodded at the Buick, "is registered to the brother of one of the escapees."

"Holy shit!"

"Please stay close by. We may need you, Miss Brannigan."

She patted Max standing beside her and wondered where the escapees might be. Then it hit her. Mr. Gallegos's chicken coop! "C'mon, Maxy," she said as she strode to Officer Sullivan.

He was huddled with three other men when she walked up: another highway patrolman, a Bernalillo County deputy sheriff, and a firefighter. She stood behind the firefighter, in Sullivan's line of sight, as he was talking. He stopped mid-sentence. "Miss Brannigan?"

"I have what may be useful information for you."

"What's that?"

All heads turned to her.

"There's a bomb shelter beneath that chicken coop." She pointed at the corner of the alfalfa field at the white frame structure. "You access it through the coop."

The four men followed the line extending from the end of her finger to the nondescript chicken coop seventy-five yards away.

"What do you know about it?" the deputy sheriff asked.

"Mr. Gallegos showed it to me one time."

"Is that his house over there?" Sullivan nodded toward the house a half block away on a large piece of land that included the alfalfa field and the chicken coop.

"Yes. He lives by himself. An adorable man. His wife died a few years ago. Kids are grown and gone." She saw Mr. Gallegos standing on his porch observing the commotion. "Want me to take you over to meet him?"

"Absolutely." Sullivan turned his attention back to the men. "You heard what Miss Brannigan said." He glanced from one man to the next. "I want everyone to stay on high alert." He pointed at the deputy sheriff. "Set up roadblocks a half mile in all directions."

"Yes, sir," the deputy replied.

He turned to the other highway patrolman. "Alert the tactical team to be on standby." Then he reached for Kelsey's arm. "Let's go see Mr. Gallegos."

Kelsey quickly ran through introductions and niceties between her next-door neighbor and the policeman, and Sullivan explained the volatile situation with the escapees and the urgent need to check out the bomb shelter.

Santiago Gallegos nodded. "I understand, Officer Sullivan, but I don't want you people to do anything to my chickens."

"We'll be extremely careful around your chickens, Mr. Gallegos, I promise."

"Maybe I'll come with you. All the chickens know me."

"It would be better if you stayed here." He glanced at Kelsey. "Maybe Miss Brannigan and her dog could come stay here with you while we perform the search."

"Max and I would like that," Kelsey said.

"We'll report back to you as soon as we're finished," Sullivan continued. "The sooner we locate and apprehend the suspects, the sooner you can both return home to peace and quiet." He turned and left.

Kelsey's eyes followed Sullivan as he hurried to his squad car while giving orders on his shoulder mic.

Mr. Gallegos sat down with an exasperated sigh on one of three metal lawn chairs on his porch. "*Bueno*, Kelsey, have a seat."

They had been chatting intermittently only a few minutes when, from the chicken coop fifty yards away, the sound of squawking chickens filled the air.

He stood and walked quickly to the end of the porch. "I asked Officer Sullivan not to scare my chickens."

Kelsey got out of her chair and walked to his side and patted his arm.

They heard the sounds of men's voices inside the coop interrupted by occasional chicken clucks.

"Bring the prisoner transport van down here!" someone shouted.

Kelsey watched the van pull away from in front of her house, then turn down her driveway and across her lot to the chicken coop on the edge of the alfalfa field, which was now surrounded by cops.

Soon she and Mr. Gallegos were staring at three handcuffed men in orange prisoner coveralls staggering toward the van's headlights.

"What the hell?" Mr. Gallegos said.

"Looks like they got 'em."

"*Parese, señora*, but it looks like they're drunk."

A lone figure emerged from the coop and headed toward the porch. Officer Sullivan. He stopped at the side of the porch. "We got 'em, folks. Passed out drunk."

"How 'bout my chickens?"

"Your chickens are fine, Mr. Gallegos. They're just fine."

24

KELSEY RAPPED ON JOHN BUSCAGLIA'S GARAGE DOOR AND OPENED IT. "Good morning, John," she called to him as he began his morning work routine at the rear of the garage.

"Hi, Kelsey!" he shouted. His voice echoed from one of the metal bins. "Welcome home!" He stood and wiped his hands on his jeans, then reached out and shook her hand. "What were all the flashing police lights over at your place last night? I could see the fuss from way over here and I was worried about you."

"It was a wild scene. Unbelievable! Two escapees from the Metropolitan Detention Center, with the help of a brother of one of them, robbed a liquor store, then headed to Corrales. One of the escapees grew up here and was a chum of my next-door neighbor's son. Mr. Gallegos's son."

"You've mentioned him before."

She took off her gloves and shoved them into her jacket pockets. "I told you about the bomb shelter."

"Under his chicken coop."

"Correct. When they were kids, his son and his escapee friend used to play hide-n-seek down there."

He put his wrists on his hips. "I'll be damned."

"Seems they tracked the two escapees to Mr. Gallegos's property and mine. There were cops and cop cars everywhere."

"Exactly what it looked like from this side of the river."

"To make a long story short, the State Police found the escapees and their accomplice brother in the bomb shelter and placed them in custody. No gunfire. No casualties. And, though they were squawking like hell, no injured chickens!"

"No one was hurt?"

"Nope. The three bad guys were passed out drunk." She laughed. "Easy to handcuff."

"The owners of that held-up liquor store should be rewarded."

John handed Kelsey one of the feed containers.

"I came across a trivia question yesterday," he said as they walked to the door.

"Let's have it."

"Are the word origins for *raven* and *ravenous* related?"

"I suspect they are." Kelsey hesitated. "Of course. They must be."

"Aha!" He stopped and placed his index finger against her shoulder. "*Raven* is from the German word *khraben*, the grating call of a raven. *Ravenous* is of Latin origin, meaning 'to consume food voraciously.' They are not related. Now, aren't you glad to know that?"

"It might win me a drink sometime."

He winked at her and grabbed the binoculars hanging by a leather strap beside the door. "We have some hungry customers waiting out there." They left the garage and walked down the path to the mews, both glancing up at the large dead cottonwood tree, hoping for signs of Midnight. "I have a hunch we may also see a visitor up on one of those high branches. Possibly two."

"That would be beyond wonderful."

They were in a raptor mew with an injured red-tailed hawk huddled in an insulated corner of the mew. "I took him in two days ago. Kept him in the house the first day. Poor fellow was hit by a light aircraft over near Double Eagle Airport west of town. The pilot followed him as he glided feebly groundward, and as soon as he landed, he notified Wildlife Rescue of the bird's location. One of our people sped over and found him unconscious but still breathing. He was bleeding from the mouth and unable to stand. I was contacted along with one of our veterinarian volunteers who, by the way, is not very optimistic about his recovery." He looked down at the hawk. "But I'm going to try my damnedest to save the old boy."

Kelsey knelt down near the injured bird. "You poor thing." She sat back, her hands resting on her legs.

"His injuries suggested head trauma, likely from colliding with the aircraft. After I brought him here I began feeding him fluids. And hoped he could rest. Before long he was lifting his head, then standing. Yesterday

I hand-fed him a defrosted mouse." John glanced around the enclosure, then pushed the bird's empty water container aside and slipped a fresh container of water beneath his beak. "Here you are, boy." The hawk began drinking. "Let me have that ground-up roadkill." He pointed to a small circular paper plate with a half cup of ground jackrabbit.

She handed the plate to him and glanced outside at the cottonwood. Two ravens were perched on one of the branches. "Look who's here," she whispered.

One of the ravens left the branch and descended to the grass below to search for breakfast.

With his free hand, John took the binoculars from around his neck and handed them to Kelsey. "Slip outside for a better look. I'll join you when I'm through here."

Kelsey placed the narrow binocular strap around her neck and stood. She opened the door and exited the mew, then walked several steps into the open field of grass. She turned to her left to the cottonwood tree, perhaps half a football field away.

She observed both ravens with the field glasses. The raven perched on the branch wore the orange leg band. Midnight! He scrutinized Kelsey for a moment, then uttered a series of undulating *quarks*.

Kelsey responded with her own *quarks* while the raven on the ground stopped foraging to take stock of its partner on the tree branch and the human calling from up the slope.

Midnight sounded two friendly, reassuring *caulk* calls. Kelsey answered.

John had finished feeding the red-tailed hawk and was standing outside the mew observing the conversation. Kelsey noticed the admiring look on his face.

The raven on the ground, likely a female, made a series of deep, penetrating, rasping *caws*.

Midnight, above on the branch, responded with another rasping *caw*.

"Kelsey, take a few steps toward them and give a response," John said.

She began to move forward in the ravens' direction and they flew away. "Damn!"

"That was one of the most fascinating interactions I've ever seen."

He walked to where she stood observing the birds flying east over the Rio Grande. "Even better than the last one. My spine tingled."

"I wish they hadn't left. Do you think they'll come back?"

"I have no doubt. None whatsoever. Midnight is staking out his territory."

"Really?"

"This place, your home across the river, you and me. We're all a part of it." He ran his tongue around the inside of his cheek. "And something very significant has occurred. Midnight's no longer alone. He's found a companion. He's made the transition back to freedom and joining up with other birds. Midnight's going to survive!"

Kelsey smiled and her eyes began to well. "I'm without words, John. I'm speechless."

"I am as well." He took her arm. "Let's finish feeding our other feathered friends, then go inside for a cup of coffee."

Kelsey finished her second cup of coffee and walked up John's driveway to her pickup. She strapped in, started the engine, and began driving east to her home on the other side of the Rio Grande, the same route taken by Midnight and his partner an hour earlier. From up on the hillside she could see her modest home and piece of land. Max would be in the backyard waiting for an ear scratch and a tummy rub.

She turned onto the narrow asphalt road running beside the river. When she approached the bridge, she noticed two ravens circling a thousand feet above. She continued glancing upward from time to time until she pulled into her driveway and stopped. She got out of the pickup and looked skyward. The two ravens maintained their circular pattern directly above her.

One of them *quarked*. She returned the *quark*.

〰〰〰

Two days later Kelsey joined Rick for drinks and dinner at the Frontier Bar and Grill. "Are you going to report the rest stop incident to law enforcement?" Rick asked.

"What would it accomplish? I don't know who he is, who he works for, where he lives. I only know he's a disgusting, woman-hating slob."

"You know his tractor trailer description and California plates. There might be cameras installed at those rest stops."

"I want this nightmare to end, Rick." She set down her napkin.

He placed his hand on hers. "As you wish. But the bastard had better pray I never see him or his rig."

She lifted his hand to her lips.

25

DEREK VOGEL AND TONY FUENTES PARKED THEIR SANTA FE POLICE CRUISER in the parking lot of Los Amigos Restaurant on Rodeo Road and walked the short distance to the front door for a Saturday lunch of green enchiladas.

The restaurant owner, a middle-aged Hispanic gentleman, had just seated them at a table for four in the front dining room when they saw Sally and Dix walk in. They motioned to them to join them.

Sally waved back and she and Dix made their way through the dining room to their table. Both men stood as they approached.

"Nice to see the two of you," Derek said.

"I hope we're not interrupting a business lunch," Dix replied.

"Business can wait," Tony said with a smile.

A member of the waitstaff approached wearing a black polo shirt with the restaurant logo. "What would you like to drink, folks?" Without missing a beat, he took their orders and left.

Derek turned to Sally. "Have you seen any more of that guy in the Range Rover? The one we ran a trace on?"

"As a matter of fact, I'm glad we ran into you gentlemen." She glanced at both of them. "A while back, I looked out my kitchen window after turning off the lights and saw the son of a bitch parked in front of my house. Just like he was that night you discovered him. Black Range Rover, tinted windows, no lights."

The waiter returned with their iced tea and coffee drinks, then took their orders for lunch: Two green chile enchiladas, a bowl of chile stew, and a BLT.

Sally awaited a response. The police officers said nothing, so she continued. "I got spooked. Almost contacted the two of you, but realized this is my baby to deal with, not yours." She placed the straw between her lips and took a sip of iced tea. "First thing the next morning, I contacted a private investigator here in town. Gentleman named Holmes. He jumped right on it." She glanced down at the checkered tablecloth. "No question about it. I'm being stalked. He has it all documented."

"What are you going to do?" Tony asked.

"I met with my attorney this morning. Just left his office. We're filing charges."

"Good for you."

"A first-time stalking offense is a misdemeanor. Second offense is a fourth degree felony."

"That's correct," Derek said. "And I don't remember, Sally, if I told you. I filed a report the night we found Brattan parked in front of your house."

"No, you didn't tell me."

"You might want to mention that to your attorney. It helps a prosecutor to have a police report on file."

"I'll tell him. Thank you."

Derek pulled a pen and his business card from his shirt pocket. He flipped the card over and wrote a telephone number on the back. "You're doing all the right things. Knowing you, I'm not surprised." He handed her the card. "Here's my personal cell number. If you ever find yourself with an immediate threat, call me. Tony and I are usually together. One of us will respond. If we're off duty when you call, I or someone else will be at your place pronto."

"There's something else I want you both to know." She looked from one to the other. "I've advised my attorney." She patted Dix's wrist. "And Dix knows." She paused. "I carry a loaded Smith & Wesson .38 in an ankle holster."

The two cops glanced at each other.

"You got a permit?" Derek asked.

"Yup."

"You have the holster on now?"

"Yes, I do."

Tony looked at Derek.

"That adds a new dimension to things, doesn't it?" Derek said.

Tony nodded. "As our friend, Sally, would say, 'Yup.'" He smirked.

Sally stared at Tony "In all due respect, this is no laughing matter. Jake Brattan is dangerous. If he threatens me again and help is not right there, I'll shoot the bastard."

"I apologize, Sally," Tony said. "I know the guy's a threat. Just be careful."

"Have either of you run a background check on him?"

"Yeah." Derek sat back. "Not much we can tell you, though."

"Why not?"

"There's nothing high profile," Derek said. "Doing drugs, but not dealing. Working for a well-heeled brothel owner in Pahrump, Nevada. Pimping for high rollers in the region." He flexed his jaw muscles. "He covers his tracks pretty well. Nothing we can nail him with."

"Yet," Tony added.

∞∞∞∞∞

Sal Zimmer's refrigerated trailer was freshly loaded with produce from central Arizona's farmlands when he pulled into the Flying J Travel Center on Interstate 40 west of Albuquerque. His right hand rested on the gearshift. Tattooed on the back of the hand was the swastika.

An 18-wheeler with a national moving and storage company pulled up beside him on his left. He glanced with envy at the large sleeper cab and visualized all the comforts of home it must contain: small kitchen area, comfortable bunk, maybe a shower. The driver stepped down from the other side and began walking toward the station. It was a woman driver.

Sal was several steps behind her when he called out, "Hey, woman driver!"

She turned her head and glanced over her shoulder but didn't stop.

"Hey, woman driver, I'm talking to you!" He quickened his pace and grabbed her shoulder. "Goddam bitch, I'm talking to you!" he spat out.

The woman let out a scream. "Danny, help me!"

Sal slapped her across the face and heard a truck door slam behind him, but paid no attention to it. "You goddam women drivers are taking our jobs! Get your sorry asses the hell out of our rigs!" His right fist went into motion to strike her again when an arm made of iron wrapped around his neck and he collapsed on the ground.

26

SALLY, STILL IN HER WORK SHIRT AND JEANS, FINISHED DRYING THE DINNER dishes and flipped the kitchen light switch off. She glanced outside through the narrow window beside the switch and saw a black Range Rover enter the cul-de-sac at a high rate of speed then jump the curb in front of a neighbor's house. It came to an out-of-control stop beneath the streetlight in front of her home. The headlights went off, the driver's side door opened, and Jake Brattan stepped out.

Sally froze.

Jake stumbled around the rear of the car. In his right hand he carried a liquor bottle. He leaned back against the car, tilted his head, took a healthy swig, and wiped his mouth on the sleeve of his sport coat. He staggered toward the house and tripped on the concrete curb, falling face first onto the sidewalk. The glass liquor bottle shattered into a thousand pieces.

Sally turned and ran down the hallway to her bedroom and grabbed the cell phone from the top of the nightstand and the holstered snub-nosed .38 from the drawer. She sat on the edge of the bed and strapped on the ankle holster, then punched Derek Vogel's phone number on the cell phone.

She held the phone against her ear as she ran back down the hallway to the living room and stood in the dark at the side of the front window. Jake was picking himself up off the sidewalk.

Derek answered the phone. "Vogel here."

"Derek, this Sally Tremaine. I need your help. Fast. Jake Brattan is in my front yard." Her voice tensed. "Drunk."

Jake stopped in the middle of the front yard, a mix of flagstone, gravel, and desert plants. He unzipped his pants and urinated on one of the plants.

"Is anyone with him?"

"He's by himself."

"Tony and I are ten minutes from your house. We're on our way. We'll check for any other units closer to you. Don't hang up. Keep the line open. I'm putting the phone on speaker."

"Ten-four." Sally slipped her cell phone into a shirt pocket.

She watched Jake zip his pants and stagger to the front door.

In the distance she heard a police siren. She moved from the living room window to the stuffed chair at the end of the living room with an unobstructed view of the front door entryway.

He began pounding on the door. "Sally Tremaine, you bitch, I know you're in there. Open the goddamn door!"

She pulled the cell phone from her shirt pocket to make certain it was on—and relaying Jake's drunken screams to Derek Vogel. "I hope Derek's recording this," she whispered, returning the phone to the pocket.

She sat in the stuffed chair, waiting, then she pulled the .38 from its holster and felt a slight tremor in her hands.

Brattan pounded his fists against the door. "Goddamn you, open the fucking door!"

Sally clicked the .38 off safety and held it with both hands, prepared to raise it in an instant. In her peripheral vision, she picked up neighbors' lights being turned on. The police siren drew closer. She heard a second siren closing from the opposite direction.

Suddenly the entire house became a cacophony of shattering wood, broken glass, and falling plaster as Jake Brattan body-slammed the front door, crashing onto the tile entryway floor and landing on his back. The only light on his sweating, drunken body was a faint shadowy light from the streetlight outside. He attempted to roll to his side.

"Stay where you are, you son of a bitch!" Sally shouted. "I've got a .38 aimed right at your fucking eardrum!"

He turned his head to the side. His body remained motionless while his watery eyes searched for her. Then he went limp.

The sirens turned silent. She turned to see one city police car speed into the cul-de-sac, stopping directly in front of the Range Rover while another unit blocked the entryway. Two policemen, weapons drawn, ran down the sides of the house toward the back.

"Sally, are you there?" Derek's voice came from the cell phone in her shirt pocket.

"Affirmative." She glanced at Jake Brattan's body for any sign of movement. There was none.

"We have your house surrounded. You okay?"

"I'm okay." Her voice wavered. "I'm holding the .38 on the bastard. He's passed out in the entryway. The son of a bitch broke my front door down."

"Stay put. Tony and I are coming in."

"Ten-four."

Brattan's body remained still. Sally returned the revolver safety switch to safe and lowered her tired, aching hands to her lap.

Derek and Tony dashed into the shattered entryway, patted Jake Brattan down, rolled him over, and cuffed him.

She saw Tony breathing heavily. "Derek," he said, "that was way too easy. This dude's more than passed out."

"You got that right." He glanced across the living room, then back at Tony.

Tony placed his index and middle fingers against Jake's carotid artery. "He's got no pulse."

"Check for wounds," Derek said as he stood and walked across the living room to Sally.

"Thank you, Derek." She looked up. "I'm exhausted."

He reached for the revolver on her lap. "I hate to do this, Sally, but I have to." He lifted the snub-nosed .38 and disengaged the cylinder. All five rounds were there. No shots had been fired. He smelled the weapon for evidence of burned gunpowder and returned it to her. "Put it back in your holster."

<hr />

"INTRUDER DIES IN WOMAN'S HOME," read the article headline in the Santa Fe newspaper. It continued, "Jake Brattan, an ex-prison inmate and out-of-state resident, died of an apparent heart attack while breaking into the southside Santa Fe home of Sally Tremaine."

Sally set the newspaper on Vicky's desk when she arrived at the office two days after the break-in. "I've been successful thus far in declining all interview requests from television stations and newspapers, Vicky, but I don't know how long my luck can last."

Vicky glanced down at the newspaper. "Do you think reporters might call here at the office? Looking for you and an interview?"

"I think that's very likely. But you and I have a business to run and trucking schedules to maintain." She sat in the chair beside Vicky's desk. "I spent most of yesterday at police headquarters in Santa Fe and with my lawyer. They all understand our situation. Fully."

"Can we refer queries to your lawyer?"

"Yes. He's fully prepared." Sally stood. "That son of a bitch, Jake Brattan, God rest his evil soul, is going to haunt me until this all blows over. It may take a few months or even a year, but we can handle it."

Vicky walked around her desk and hugged Sally. "You bet your sweet ass we can!"

With that, they both broke out laughing. Laughed until there were tears in their eyes.

Sally wiped her eyes with a handkerchief. "I needed that!" She reached forward and patted Vicky on the cheek. "Bet your sweet ass I did!"

"So did I, boss. We've all been worried about you. The Doc Morgan trucker bunch as well as the folks at Atchison. Running this business is a challenge in itself. Having to also keep looking over your shoulder for a stalker is way too much."

Sally glanced up at the scheduling board on the wall behind Vicky. Nothing was scheduled for Atchison Industries until a Salt Lake City delivery the middle of the following week. There were only a few local or regional runs for other clients in the interim. "Dix has family visiting from Beaumont."

"I know," Vicky said.

"Kelsey and I had a good visit on the phone last night. She's having fun with her raven."

Vicky grinned. "She's so proud of that bird. You'd think she was Midnight's mama."

"I think I'll give her a call this morning. See if she wants to drive up to Chama for a couple of days."

"Chama?"

"A trucker from up there called me. He's interested in Doc's rig and wants to see it next time he's in Albuquerque. He owns a small trucking company in Pagosa Springs, fifty miles north of Chama. This would be his own truck. If it works for Kelsey we might drive it up there so he can check it out."

"Excellent idea," Vicky said. "Spend a few days off the radar. If anyone drops by looking for you, I'll just tell them you're out of town."

"The gentleman's name is Zach Post. Zachary Post. If we decide we like him and think Doc would have liked him, we'll try to strike a quick win-win deal."

"Then I can drive up to get you and Kelsey and spend the night. The three of us can do the High Country Saloon for drinks and dinner and whatever else might happen."

"Sounds like a plan."

"When you talk to Kelsey, tell her there's lots of cowboys in Chama!"

"I think our girl Kelsey may have already found her cowboy."

27

Sally drove the T600 from Albuquerque to the village of Abiquiu where they stopped for a snack at Bode's Kitchen. Kelsey took the driver's seat for the remaining fifty miles while Max rode in the back seat of the cab.

As she got into the passenger seat, Sally picked up the Albuquerque newspaper Kelsey had been reading. A small article on the front page, dateline Albuquerque, was circled. Beside it was a large exclamation point. She read:

> *Salvatore Zimmer, a trucker from Indio, California, suffered a broken neck at the Pilot truck stop off of Interstate 40 yesterday, on Albuquerque's west side. Witnesses said Zimmer had physically attacked the wife of another trucker who came to the defense of his wife. The wife, also a trucker, is hospitalized with facial fractures. Her husband will not be charged. Charges, however, are pending against assailant Zimmer who is on life support.*

"Did you know this Salvatore Zimmer, Kelsey?"

"He was the guy who, a couple of years ago in Pine Bluff, was on my case for being a woman trucker and Buffalo Bill Gentry kicked his ass. Sounds like he was nailed for taking on another woman driver."

"Thank God her husband was there."

"I never told you about it, Sally, but he came after me again on my recent Manhattan, Kansas run. At a rest stop. I gave the bastard a face full of Mace."

"Good God, Kelsey, you must tell me about these things! Have you told Rick?"

"I told him. He's ready to kill the asshole. I'll give him the article when we get back home."

Sally rested her hand on Kelsey's shoulder. "Please be careful, Kelsey. I'm glad you've got Max."

"I am, too. I count my blessings every day for my little warrior."

"As you should."

They were heading north on Highway 84, just beginning a climb to a plateau overlooking the Chama River. Kelsey patted the steering wheel. "Doc Morgan took good care of this rig."

"It was his baby. He bought it the day he passed his Commercial Driver's License test. He'd closed his medical practice shortly before that. A very successful medical practice, I understand. He was pursuing his dream."

"When did Vicky join him?"

"Vicky and her family, from Santo Domingo Pueblo, were patients of Doc's. Vicky impressed Doc with her energy and her intelligence. When he learned she was at the top of her class in bookkeeping, he offered her a job with Doc Morgan Trucking. She's been with the company ever since. That girl is smart as a whip, as you've seen since you joined us, and she's extremely loyal to the company and to all of us."

"I suspect her loyalty to Doc is still a part of her life." Kelsey pulled to the left to pass a slow-moving early model Dodge pickup.

"Very much so. They were devoted to each other. Doc treated Vicky like a daughter. Did you see her face when we pulled his rig out of the lot?"

Kelsey sat back in her seat, her fingers loose on the bottom of the steering wheel. "I saw a tear on its way. She'll miss looking out the office window and seeing it."

"She's counting on us to sell to the right owner/driver," Sally said.

"Zachary Post?"

"He sounds good on the telephone. We'll see."

The Rivers Crossing Lodge on Chama's south side was perfect for their needs. Nice rooms and plenty of parking with maneuvering room for the tractor and trailer. A message awaited Sally when she checked in at the front desk: "Sally, give me a call after you and your partner settle in. I'll drive over to see the T600. Zach." His phone number was written at the bottom of the note.

"Zach Post is delivering a certified check to me in the morning, Vicky." Sally stood on the long front porch of the motel, holding the cell phone against her ear. "So, come on up and get Kelsey and me."

"Did he like Doc's truck?"

"He fell in love with it. Checked it inside and outside, opened the hood to examine the engine. He covered every square inch of the truck. Been looking for one just like it for years."

"Did you get your asking price?"

"No, but he made what I thought was a reasonable counteroffer and we shook hands. Doc would like him and I know he'll take good care of the truck. Have any reporters dropped by looking for me?"

"There've been three. An Albuquerque newspaper, a Santa Fe paper, and a TV station. Told 'em all you were out of town. They tried to press me, but I wouldn't budge."

"Thanks, Vicky. I owe you a drink when you get up here."

"I'll take it, boss. By the way, my mom will come in to cover the office phones while I'm gone."

"Bless your mother."

"I'll tell her you said that. See you mañana."

"Ten-four."

No sooner had Sally returned the cell phone to her pocket than it rang again. "Hello?"

"Hi, Sally. This is Buffalo Bill Gentry."

Kelsey, Sally, and Vicky sat at a table near the bar at the High Country Saloon. The jukebox at the rear of the saloon belted out country and western with patrons rolling their quarters down the slot for oldies like "Big Bad John" and "Abilene."

Kelsey got up from the table and walked to the bar for a second round. The portly bartender handed her three bottles of Coors with a grin, then pulled out a towel and wiped a section of the old mahogany bar before turning to another customer for a refill order.

"Do you take tips?" Vicky asked as she set the bottles on the table.

"Look at this gal." Sally reached for one of the bottles. "Were you a waitress in an earlier life?"

Kelsey laughed. "Never a waitress or a barmaid, but, ladies, in Uncle Sam's Army you learn to do many things. One of those things is carrying beer bottles."

Sally pulled her key ring out of her pocket to clip a hangnail with the clipper. She glanced at the bearded St. Christopher medal beside the clipper, the medal given to her by Father Pat at Devils Tower. "This is miles off the subject," she said, "but I want you both to know I had a telephone conversation with a nice bearded gentleman just before we came over here. Bill Gentry."

Kelsey lit up. "Really! Handsome Buffalo Bill with his distinguished white beard?"

"He's going to be joining Doc Morgan Trucking."

"Sally, this is beyond wonderful!" Kelsey's eyes danced. "Buffalo is my world's favorite trucker. Ever since he got Max and me out of the jam with that asshole in Pine Bluff. Oh, my God!" She raised her bottle of Coors in toast. "I don't know what you said to him or how you did it. This is fabulous!"

"We'll be back to full staff." She rubbed St. Chris with her thumb as she returned the key ring to her pocket

In the background, the jukebox played Tammy Wynette and "Stand by Your Man."

After they gave their dinner orders to a young waiter with Elvis Presley hair, Sally pushed her chair back. Think I'll visit the ladies' room."

"Don't get lost," Vicky said, taking a swallow of beer.

As Sally approached the door to the ladies' room, the door to the men's room across the narrow hallway swung open and a cowboy walked out. Behind him, standing at a urinal, a grizzled old cowpuncher lifted his hat in greeting with his free hand and nodded to her. She nodded back at him and continued to the ladies' room.

After she returned to the table, the old-timer walked over from the bar. He attempted a greeting with his raspy voice, but the racket of people talking, dishes colliding, drunken laughter, and kitchen staff yelling at each other drowned out whatever words he mumbled. He moseyed back to his tall stool at the bar.

In the distance Johnny Cash sang, *Don't take your guns to town, son.*

28

THE SUN HAD JUST CRESTED THE TIPS OF THE SANDIAS AND KELSEY WAS sound asleep after arriving home from the Chama trip late the night before. Max was curled up on his blanket at the foot of the bed. Suddenly they were jolted awake by the harsh bedlam of squawking ravens and wailing coyotes coming from the direction of Mr. Gallegos's chicken coop.

Kelsey sprang out of bed and ran to the back porch with Max at her heels.

Two coyotes were trapped in the chicken-wire fenced yard behind the chicken coop and were being aerially assaulted and yelled at by Midnight and his partner. The terrified animals had burrowed an entry beneath the fence to feast on chicken, oblivious to the two raven sentinels nearby, and were now trapped inside the pen.

One of the animals managed to crawl back through the narrow opening and fled to safety at warp speed while the coyote still entrapped snapped at the two ravens and wailed with each claw or beak dug into its back. Soon it also broke free and followed in pursuit of its mate.

"Señora, everybody has to eat," Santiago Gallegos said to Kelsey as they stood outside the white wood-frame chicken coop. "I just don't want *esos coyotes* eating my chickens." He glanced at the chicken pen, then back at Kelsey. "I have been watching these two *cuervos*, the ravens, for several days while you been at work driving your big truck. They spend more time here when you are home. I think they live someplace near here. But they been protecting my chickens. Yesterday they chased away a hawk!" He smiled a big toothy smile. "Because they think the chickens are *yours*." He laughed. "I think they have . . . how you say it . . . 'adopted' you, Señora."

"Mr. Gallegos, I've been working with a very kind man across the river, John Buscaglia. He lives up the hill." She pointed to John's property in the distance. "The big raven, I call him Midnight, was injured in a storm near Taiban, in eastern New Mexico. Mr. Buscaglia has helped the raven recover. So, really, Midnight and his partner have adopted both Mr. Buscaglia and me."

"Señora, you got a name for the partner?"

"No, I don't. I don't know if it's a male or a female."

"What about Moses? Midnight and Moses! You like that? It's like the song, 'Moonlight and Roses'!" He tilted his head back and laughed.

She let out a whoop. "Mr. Gallegos, we'll name the partner Moses!"

"Please call me Santiago. We been friends and *vecino* neighbors a long time. And I'll call you Kelsey. *Esta bien?*"

"*Esta bien*, Santiago." She reached out and hugged him.

"*Bueno.*" He smiled. "That makes me happy and it makes my chickens happy." He turned to the south. "I think Midnight and Moses must live down by the river someplace, or maybe over in the Sandias. But they like to come over here in the daytime to hang out with us. *Que no?*"

She laughed. "*Que si*, Santiago."

Perched on the branch of a cottonwood tree not far away, the two ravens exchanged gurgling sounds. Then Midnight let out a *quark*. Kelsey responded. The conversation continued with Santiago and Max turning their heads from Midnight to Kelsey and back again.

By now, the chickens were beginning to emerge from the coop, one at a time, confident the coyotes were nowhere around.

Kelsey glanced down at the hole dug beneath the fence by the coyotes. "Can I help you repair the fence?"

"No thank you, Kelsey." He surveyed the damage. "I'll go get my tools and fix it. You and Max got work to do."

Her cell phone rang. She pulled it from her shirt pocket. "Hi, John. How's it going?"

"Kelsey, I haven't seen the two ravens for a few days. Have you seen them?"

"I'm looking at them right now. They're perched on a fence railing a short distance away. Mr. Gallegos and I had some excitement this morning. I'll drive over in a little bit and tell you about it."

"I just finished the morning feed. I'll put the coffeepot on. I can use your help in banding a bald eagle."

"John, do you remember the song 'Moonlight and Roses'?"

"Of course. A classic."

"Mr. Gallegos just named Midnight's partner, Moses."

John was silent for a moment. "Midnight and Moses! Get on over here!"

Kelsey held the bald eagle in her arms while John attached the leg band. It was an orange-colored band like Midnight's. The eagle struggled to get free. "I can see why you asked me to help. This young fellow is anxious to leave."

"There, I've got it." He exhaled. "Put the bird down on the table so he can cool off. Then we'll swing open the front of the mew and release him."

"*Caulk-caulk-caulk-caulk.*"

Kelsey and John turned and looked up at the dead cottonwood at the rear of the yard. There they perched, Midnight and Moses. Kelsey answered, "*Caulk-caulk-caulk-caulk.*"

"Let's go outside," he said.

John followed Kelsey to the open grass area where they stopped, looking up at the two ravens.

"*Caulk-caulk,*" Kelsey spoke first.

"*Caulk-caulk-caulk-caulk,*" Midnight answered, flexing his wings with each call. He turned his head from side to side, dropped from the cottonwood branch, and slipped into a glide to the top of a tree stump a few feet from Kelsey and John. The top of the stump was but a few inches above the ground. He uttered a series of relaxed, friendly *caulk* calls. Kelsey responded as best she could.

Midnight stretched and flapped his wings, then turned and gazed in different directions. He preened, stretched again, and picked at twigs beside the stump . . . then he began a series of soft chuckles and gurgling sounds. He followed with what appeared to be a bow and a thank you, then launched into the air and flew east toward the Sandia Mountains. Moses left the cottonwood branch and followed him.

29

KELSEY AND RICK SAT ON KELSEY'S BACK PORCH IN THE LATE AFTERNOON a few months later. Max and Molly rested at their feet.

Kelsey's eyes wandered across the backyard to Santiago's chicken coop and the memory of Midnight and Moses chasing the two coyotes out of the pen.

"Caulk-caulk-caulk-caulk."

They both looked up. The dogs awakened from their snooze. In one of the cottonwoods behind Santiago's house sat Midnight and Moses. Below them, foraging in the grass, were four raven youngsters.

"My God, Rick, would you look at that! Midnight and Moses brought their kids over to see us."

"They sure did. What a sight!"

"How cool!" She clasped her hands on her lap and turned to him, noticing the outline of something square in his shirt pocket.

"This reminds me of something I've been meaning to ask you, Kelsey." He reached into his shirt pocket and pulled out a little black box. He flipped it open to a stunning diamond ring. "Will you marry this old cowboy?"

She stared at the ring and broke out in a radiant, romantic smile, then rose from her chair and sat on his lap, facing him. "Why hell yes, I will!" They wrapped their arms around each other in a delicious embrace.

Acknowledgments

Very special thanks to:

Bill Araujo – Freelance photographer and docent, Kansas City Zoo

Jim Battaglia – Wildlife Rehabilitator, Wildlife Rescue, Inc. of
New Mexico

Hugh Cook – Teacher, Writer, Editor, Ancaster, Ontario, Canada

Ross Crandall – Research Biologist, Craighead Beringa South,
Kelly, Wyoming

Brady Griffith – Lieutenant, Field Operations, New Mexico
Department of Game & Fish

Kathy Harris - Doctor of Veterinary Medicine, Albuquerque,
New Mexico

Gayle M. Kearns – Docent, Kansas City Zoo

Roberta Winchester – Wildlife Rescue, Inc. of New Mexico

TOM CLAFFEY

Tom Claffey, a member of Western Writers of America, spent his growing-up years in northern New Mexico and southern Colorado. He majored in English literature at New Mexico Military Institute and Creighton University and, in 1954, accepted an appointment to West Point. He graduated in 1958 and became a pilot in the U.S. Air Force. In civilian life he worked in investment securities and banking and began writing for publication in 1981. He lives in Santa Fe.